SPOILER

SPOILER

ACCORDING TO THE BOOK OF BEN

AMANDA PRANTERA

BLOOMSBURY

First published in Great Britain in 2003

Copyright © 2003 by Amanda Prantera

The moral right of the author has been asserted

Bloomsbury Publishing Plc, 38 Soho Square, London W1D 3HB

A CIP catalogue record for this book
is available from the British Library

ISBN 0 7475 6530 9

10 9 8 7 6 5 4 3 2 1

Typeset by Hewer Text Ltd, Edinburgh
Printed in Great Britain by Clays Ltd, St Ives plc

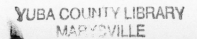

To H.G.
my friend who fell

OUT OF THE DEPTHS

Norwich, 2002

You're a literary laddie, Ben, says my analyst Dr Macpherson. Put it all down on paper. Set your thoughts in order that way. The writing cure works, you know, it's as old as Adam.

It can't be the Scottish accent, as he's hardly got one, but sometimes I think it's only because he uses words like wee and laddie that I pay any heed to McShrink whatsoever. Old as Adam. Adam barely made it to *twenty* blanking *seven*. Call that old? The child only reached fifteen – and that's *days* we're talking about here, not years, not months, not even measly weeks. *Fifteen, pathetic, blameless days.* When and if I'm ever granted the Beatific Vision, and to whichever end I'm granted It: frazzlement or prize, I'm not going to swoon or turn away or even blink if I can help it, I'm going to stare It straight on and say, along with Diderot or d'Holbach or whichever of those feisty *Philosophes* it was, How DARED You, God? How dared You create a world where such things happen? Answer me that one, All-Knowing, All-Caring, All-Permitting and All-Squandering Deity, How did You, did You DARE?

This momentous meeting, however, if it lies anywhere, lies in the future. In the meantime here comes some writing for McShrink: a couple of letters and the first five pages of my Roman scrapbook, long since scrapped. (And a good thing too. *Only* good thing, in fact, to come out of all this shambles.)

BEFORE THE FALL

PONTIFICAL COLLEGE SAINT THOMAS MORE

VIA MONTE MADAMA 14 – ROMA 00135

October 5th/6th, 2000

Dear Mum,

Here I am at last, and the above address is proof. I feel peaceful but exhausted, like a carrier pigeon that's made it across a battlefield. From my bedroom I can see - sadly not the dome of Saint Peter's (maybe from the roof, maybe in daylight, or maybe we didn't read the prospectus right) but a very fascinating modern white building, all ringed around by trees, that I swear is almost as beautiful. I have stood at the window for the past ten minutes, gazing down on it and muttering to myself, Rome, Rome, Rome, and trying not to add things like 'the Eternal City' and 'the Heart of Christendom', and failing. It's awesome and a privilege and a reward beyond my merits - you will understand. Why I've been chosen, with so many other worthier candidates to hand, I just can't imagine.

Don't go bragging, I beg of you. I got a letter from Aunt Cath just before I left in which she speaks of me rather ominously as a 'high flier'. Where did she get this notion from if not from you? I'm not that sort of a creature and you know it - at most I'm a carrier pigeon that gets where it does by luck and dint of flapping: the only high flying I can hope to do is in the spiritual direction, closer to God.

Goodnight, my dearest mum. Good morning now. Tomorrow - today - I'll try and look out a postcard of the college for you. It'll be quicker and better than trying to describe it. Forgive me, but I'm a bit done in after the journey and need to get some sleep. Keep me in your prayers as I do you in mine,

yr loving son,

Ben.

PONTIFICAL COLLEGE SAINT THOMAS MORE

VIA MONTE MADAMA 14 – ROMA 00135

Half-past midnight, Friday, October 6th.

Benedict to James: Greetings, you old turd of Satan. And take a look at this letter heading. Oh yes, everything's dead posh here, and dead modern as well, not a bit like the old brother institution with its Scutari wards and Alcatraz latrines. How's your billet in that respect? Bet it's no four-star pitch like this one here.

Nota bene that this is not a proper letter: you will get one of those later. Of a sort. This is merely an information tag, such as you might tear off the leg of a carrier pigeon: a chit to tell you of my whereabouts and furnish you with an address, should you feel like writing to your one-time buddy in his biennium of exile.

Anyway I've decided that whether you do or don't, I'm going to write to you a lot - although not always punctually and not always directly. Remember that weird scrapbook affair we read last year for German, by someone called Brinkmann who was here in Rome on a kind of artistic sabbatical in the 1970s? You know, the one with the smutty pictures that old Father M. got so tied up about when he tried to comment on them? Well, I know it was a bitter and misanthropic work in some ways but I found it dead, dead impressive and I've decided to copy Brinkmann's idea and do something like it. A testimonial. An X-ray of a place, a life, a time. In vitro veritas. If I can bring it off, that is, and if I can find the time from studies. Letters, bus tickets, postcards, innermost thoughts, impressions, the odd map or two, anything and everything that comes my way - in it'll all go like rags into a ragbag, hopefully acquiring a pattern of its own as it builds up. And then, on the eve of my noviciate, I will send the whole thing off to you as a memento. Probably with an injunction to burn it to ashes, and, equally probably, a secret hope that you won't obey. That's the only way art can be created, I think, if it is to escape the slur of vanity: in a transitory fashion, under sentence of its own death.

Oh yes, I've matured on quite a lot of points, mon cher. Vale, toodloo and arrivederci,

B.

* * *

Rome, October 6th, 2000. 1 a.m.

And now to myself and my ragbag and my private thoughts. Stick air ticket here, I think, when I get the glue.

☐

First impressions on leaving the airport: wetness, stickiness of atmosphere, unholy, not to say diabolical, noise.

Swearing of taxi driver all along the route - expressions so novel as to constitute an art form almost - and then his rather touching double take when we fished up where we did. It's early to generalise, but I think this mixture of respect and disdain for the sacred is going to be a characteristic of the city. The ad hoardings are incredibly fleshy in style, most of them, and then you come across one - maybe for underwear or something - with a graffito scrawled across it in huge black letters, DIO C'E: God exists. Brinkmann noticed that aspect of the Italian scene; I noticed it too. It really touched me, I found it really -

Interruption. The bloke next door came in to make arrangements about using the bathroom. It lies between our rooms and we have to share. Father Blaise, known, of course, as Pascal, apparently insists on both doors being locked while the bathroom is in use, but my neighbour - Scot, name of Adam - says this is just a silly nuisance: A shoots bolt on B's side, forgets, goes off to bed, and B is left shut out of his own lav. He suggests we leave both doors unlocked at all times and just warn each other with a knock.

'It's intended as a Brake on our Lusts,' he says in a capital-letter voice and then, switching to a very lower-case one, 'I'm not a homosexual, at least not so as you'd notice. And you?'

I search for a suitably laid back answer, but before I can find one he is gone. Weird fellow. V. sophisticated.

Creative urge gone too. Think I'll forget about lauds and hit the sack. Skip teeth maybe, and use the lav in the corridor. In these pages it's my intention to keep a kind of *spiritual diary as well - intense, reflective, addressed to myself alone, definitely to be removed before sending to James. Baring of soul, ruthless examination of conscience etc., even reportage on dreams. But quite honestly, I seem to have lost touch with that part of myself tonight: first I was too keyed up, and now I'm just too kippered. One more quick peep at that fascinating, spectral building on the hillside down below, and then, Buona notte, Roma, caput mundi.*

*   *   *

There, I hope that keeps McShrink happy. Although I suppose from the therapy point of view he really wants me to come up with new material instead of using stuff I've already got. But I don't see why I shouldn't do a bit of both. Energy-saving, and rather interesting – to see what I wrote at the time. And to some ends indispensable. My mood, for example. My mood of two years back. By no amount of shrivelling the imagination could I possibly recapture that, even if I wanted to. Today it's another Ben writing, describing another world: a world that spins, and how, but no longer on an axis. Just a slosh of particles and *basta*. I could say I was green, I was full of hope, of ignorance, of illusions, but these plain descriptive sentences would never give the authentic Ben of Then flavour the way the original text does.

Adam too, the first impressions – those are better hot off the block. My fear, my fascination, my twitching over his homosexual tendencies (which will spark off some really farcical entries later on – I'll include one of those later when I find the one I want). Then there's the amount of space he occupies, from the very first moment he steps on the scene. That, plus the fact that after his crushing advice there are no more letters included, either to Mum or anyone else. Shame in a way because I remember writing her a long one structured like a Breughel banquet – full of portraits of each member of the Community as they gathered in the refectory, from the Rector downwards. Or outwards, seeing as he liked to pass as a democrat. That would have been interesting to read again. A bit like having St Peter's souvenir snapshot of the Last Supper. Spot the traitor. Which is he? Get your specs out. Is it Pascal's dogsbody, Michael – that small figure in the background, bustling round the doorway in true sheepdog style, herding in the latecomers, snapping at their heels and woofing? (Pity about those beaver teeth of his, or the canine resemblance would have been complete.) Is it Father Lawrence, the massive third-year theology tutor, planted in front of that plate of spaghetti, downing it as if by vacuum principle? Is it the fastidious Father Simon, my confessor for a while, sitting watching him on the far side of the table, his aristo face oh-so-eloquently blank? Or is it gentle old Father Hildebrand, down in the right-hand corner of the frame, playing tiddlywinks on the tabletop with his heart pills? Could be any of them. Could be any combination. Could be all. Forty-two faces, forty-two skulls housing forty-two inscrutable brains with how many trillions of ideas inside? Sifting through haystacks would have been a cinch in comparison. No wonder it took me so long to find my Judas.

And now for another scrap of scrapbook.

*   *   *

Rome, October 6th, 2000, Early evening.

Re-reading last night's entries I find three pigeon metaphors. That is bad, but I'm not going to correct or rewrite. Ever. In a text like this it's the truth and spontaneity that count. Once you start getting self-conscious, you've lost it, whatever it is you had or might have had. I wonder if Brinkmann corrected his stuff?

Probably did, probably crafted no end. And probably he was right, and in the end it's actually less vain to craft than it is to presuppose that what you unreflectingly churn out is ipso facto going to possess –

Oh, hell, I'm always getting into these self-tied knots. Humility is terrible that way: you aim for it, and once you think you've got it you've ipso facto lost it.

Two ends, two ipso factos and two lost its. Hell, hell, hell. Stick with facts, Benedetto, as my new tutor calls me. Be a simple chronicler and to hell with the rest. Five hells in six lines. Just look at that – five. And now SIX.

Things done: shamefully few. This place is more like a hotel than a seminary. People are coming and going all the time; the rule of silence is waived on so many counts it's practically suspended; nobody seems to notice if you keep it or not, or if you attend office or not, or what you do. It's going to take a lot of self discipline to keep myself in line. Two gates down the road there's an American seminary in comparison with which this one is grottsville. They've got tennis courts and squash courts and human hamster-wheels galore, and we students have a standing invitation to make use of them. Lucky they don't have a swimming pool as well, or else, with this heat, it'd be lilos and iced lollies for me and Ciao tutti.

Anyway, today I went to the Gregoriana – or the Pontificia Università Gregoriana to give it its full title, I'll call it the Greg in these pages – with two other tadpoles like myself. We collected our faculty programmes and learned the bus routes and what have you, and where to buy tickets, which is usually tobacco shops. The other tads' names: Kevin and Inigo. Every time Inigo went through a

12

door before me I had to check myself from saying 'Inigo', but I got the giggles all the same, just thinking about it. I suspect he knew what was going through my mind. Perhaps it would have been better to have come out and said it. Why didn't I? Because he's black, that's why. Must try to erase this silly anti-racist angst from my character as, like humility, it ends up defeating itself. Must also look up the exact meaning of 'Risu inepto res ineptior nulla est,' which is what Inigo quoted at me in the third doorway. Sounded a bit snappy to me. (Yes, it was, I've just looked: 'Nothing more foolish than foolish laughter.')

Must also stick in p.c. of the Greg, and a photocopy of paras 1 & 2 of the syllabus as ghastly reminder of what is required of us on the language front. (Although, mind you, Kevin says he knows a guy who did a six-year doctorate stint here and could only say, 'Cuppa cheeno, prego,' at the end of it. How did he manage with his Greg essays? Quelle naïveté. He cheated of course: used the stock essays in the library like everyone else. What a lot I've got to learn.)

I found Brinkmann's details of prices and things, and what he ate and how many cats he saw, absolutely fascinating – they built up like a manic mosaic until Rome of the seventies was there before my eyes. Trouble is, B hated everything, and that sharpened his sight and powered his writing like a fire, whereas I like everyone and everything.

Except perhaps Adam. He awes me slightly: there's something a bit Brinkmannish about him – on instinct I would call it intellectual hauteur, but this is a hasty and probably uncharitable judgement. I've only seen him once

13

today, as I was leaving for the Greg, and he recognised me and smiled and asked me what subject I was reading, and when I said philosophy he smiled even more and said 'Ho, ho, a philowsowpher.' It's hard to read hauteur in that, but I'm sure it was there: I traced it in the smile and in the cadence of the second ho. Ho HO. What's his subject, I wonder? Canon law, I shouldn't wonder. That seems to be the one that carries the kudos round here.

Monday I start a crash course of Italian with a Signora Marcozzi, as my tutor, Don Anselmo, who is half-Italian himself - hence the Mediterranean mono-brow and the affectation of the 'Don' - says it is sadly below standard. (Whereas my Latin, which is not that brilliant either, he seems to think is fine. Phew. I asked Kevin whether what he said about the essays was true, and if so then why did I need coaching, and he looked impressed and said they may be grooming me for the Curia. Got to keep a toehold there, he says, got to have _someone_ on the spot to check what the Eyeties are up to. I wonder if he's right? A Bond role. Me? Doubt it somehow.) According to hearsay, la Marcozzi is preternaturally dashing for an outside collaborator. I'm sure I will like her as well.

Rome, philosophy, congenial company, cushy digs, attractive language teacher in the offing - what more do I want?

*   *   *

What more did I want? Silly rhetorical question, to which the only answer is: Certainly not what I got.

I was right, though: I was no Brinkmann. I don't think I need bother to give much more of this early diary. Just one more day in

14

full, and then I'll only put in bits, like the noises in the night and my homoerotic fluster, as they become relevant. For one thing, I can hardly bear to read the stuff with the knowledge I have now. (Adam's voice comes back to me here: *Are you sure that's the right way of putting it, Benthic: knowledge?*) For another, the diary tapers dreadfully as the slack Roman air makes its way into my system, and the entries get shorter and shorter and more and more laconic. For example, Christmas Day, when Adam must have already been caught up in a frantic storm of worry and activity, all I record is the ruddy menu. He on his crusade; me on a guzzle. They space out too, and by the end of January I'm only scribbling in the odd sentence, once a week or thereabouts. A few moans about overwork, a few of my tame views on the various philosophers I'm locked with, and a few of Adam's wilder comments on the same.

Here's a nice one. On the culmination of the Objective Geist:

January 16th, 2000

Hegel thought it would lead to the sublime expression of human culture, in fact according to Adam it leads to Gummo. (A bizarre film we'd just seen together on video. His choice not mine.)

Or what about this, a much earlier one? This is typical. It was about the first long thing he ever said to me, and I wrote it out word for word straight afterwards in a stew of admiration and fury. I'd said something a bit treacly about the excitement of reading philosophy – getting in touch with the great minds of the past sort of blather – and he swooped on me like a hawk:

'Philosophy isn't something you read, it's something you take. Like a purge – to unblock your noddle. Which is jammed up by too much philosophical fodder in the first place. Stop making notes like a schoolboy – X said that, Y

said that - down your draught and go. Other people's ideas shouldn't be reverenced or conned by rote, they should be USED. CHOMPED UP AND SUCKED ON AND SPAT OUT WHEN YOU'VE GOT THE JUICE, SPUCKITY SPUCK. So what if the thinkers who thought them were bigger men than we are? A nit on top of a giant's hairdo can still see further than the giant. You must take short cuts, learn by other people's mistakes, not follow them down the blind alleys but avoid the alleys altogether.'

Oh, Adam. If it was God made you that way, then I for one, and for once, think He did a good job. Camden's 'Epitaph for a Fallen Rider' could serve as yours as well: 'Between the stirrup and the ground, I mercy sought and mercy found . . .' The roof was a good deal higher than a horse. I hope you found all right. I hope you sought. But, knowing how you hated whingers, I suppose you weren't that bothered.

*   *   *

Rome, October 10th, 2000

La Marcozzi has teeth that fan out like a pleated tennis skirt and brassy hair with blackish roots. So much for the hoped for/dreaded intrusion of sensuality. I sometimes feel we Catholics of today short-change God terribly on the aesthetic front. He gives us the Alps, the sea, the blazing summer sun; what do we give Him back? Soppy ballads, clapboard churches, a watery litany, and to read it, not the Fanny Ardant of my fantasies, but a greasy pockmarked squinting old biddy with incipient beard growth. God doesn't notice things like that, goes the refrain. Doesn't He? The welder of Saturn's rings, the jewel setter of the whole night sky? Doesn't He?

16

We watched the Entrustment ceremony yesterday in Saint Peter's Square and the Fatima statue really had me worried; it was so wedding cakey. And then I was worried about having been worried - aesthetics is not quite ethics after all, although I'm not a total Kierkegaardian on this point - and I spoke about this to my new confessor, Father Simon, and he worried me even further by making what was virtually a class distinction between the 'thinkers' like ourselves and what he called the 'unquestioning faithful', pronounced as if he meant the 'great unwashed'. Plainchant and Piero della Francesca for us in our ebony choir stalls, and the Fatima hymn and pink-painted plaster for the plebs. Not a reassuring answer as it begs the very question that needles me. Think I shall have to ask to change confessors, or all this worrying will spiral Lord knows where. If it's not an unpopular move with the Rector, I think I shall choose someone from outside.

I have to write filling like that because already, a mere five days into my new life, I can see myself heading for a routine from which the famous Sunday blow-out looks as if it will be the only deviation:

Lauds
Meditation
Mass
Breakfast (Good. Fresh bread, wicked coffee.)
Bus to Greg
Lectures (So far: Propedeut, Log & Epist - all scarily abstract. Philos of Sci, Philos of Hist, Phenom and Ont, still to come.)
Bus back (just) in time for

Lunch

Half-hour dawdling in coffee room

Study till my nut cracks

Late afternoon work out chez Yanks

Vespers

Benediction

Supper

Half-hour chat in tadpoles' reading room (brew our own
coffee, result not so wicked)

More study

Compline (usually DIY)

and flake out on

Bed

And that's it until we start our pastoral work outside the
college, but that won't be for months yet. In the meantime
I think I will soon abandon this opus project - it's getting
a bit egocentric - and just stick in scraps and copies of
letters.

And not all of them either. Adam came in last night to
borrow shoe polish (unworthy thought but it crossed my
mind it might be for inhaling: the only shoes I've seen him
wear are trainers), and I don't know what came over me -
a desire to impress, or the need to seem not quite as boring
as I think he thinks I am - but I found myself telling him
all about my writing ambitions and even showing him
what I've done so far.

This is probably one of my reasons for stopping. He read
through in silence, batting his pale Boris Becker eyelashes,
and his mouth tilted up sideways, higher and higher, as
he read. Only the left side. Extraordinary, the style he

manages to stamp on every little thing he does. Apart from Monsignor Freeman, who used to pronounce all his Latin like he was Pavarotti and put me in mind, for some reason, of velvet, he is the only really stylish priest I have ever met. Or future priest, that is: he leaves here for his noviciate in July.

'Brinkmann,' he said when he'd finished, pocketing my tube of neutral polish as well as the black. 'Rolf Dieter. Hater of modernity, run over by a car - that's about the most inspiring thing about him, no? His mode of death?'

I find conversation with this sort of person nerve-racking and hard on the muscles, like being in a bumper-car. I tried to explain my fascination with Brinkmann - the abrasive ascetic conscience, the iconoclastic stance vis-à-vis the idols of the consumer society, including the mega-idol of democracy itself - but even as I spoke the fascination seemed to blanch and wither away.

Adam listened, still as a hare. His silences are challenging too. Although, in this case, it was mainly on account of the fact that he seemed to be listening _for_ something, and not inside the room but out of it. I had to work for his attention. 'I see,' he said, when I'd finished, and hopped off the table where he'd been sitting, no, perching - he's not a sitter, he's an alighter. 'Well, if this guy fails you, I could always step in as substitute iconoclast. Oh, yes, baby Benjamin, I could break some idols for you, I guarantee I could. I could break your priestly heart.'

Then, halfway through the door to the bathroom, he craned back again. 'By the way,' he said, 'that white building's the football stadium, Dio c'è means there's a drug dealer in the neighbourhood, and, none of my business, but if I were you I wouldn't copy in any more of those letters to Mum.'

I'm so slow-witted I didn't have time to stifle my 'Oh' or even tell him it was Benedict, actually. Roll on July, is all I can say. Forgive me, Lord, for questioning Your recruitment policy but what's a creep like that doing in a seminary? Break my priestly heart. He's the one whose heart needs the glue pot. Talk about Fragmented Man.

THE DAY THAT THOU
EATEST THEREOF THOU
SHALT SURELY DIE

It's terrible how casually stated words boomerang on you. I have indeed never seen anyone so fragmented as Adam was in that chapel, and hope I never shall again. Love is something bodies do, I know that now for sure. *MATTER thinks, Benison,* he used to say to me sometimes when he was in one of his picador moods and wanted to goad me. *Minds do sweet FA, minds are nothing – dimensionless polythene bags to help us sort out the thoughts from the farts. We have developed out of sludge, out of the primeval cosmic stockpot and we are PART of it, brains and all. MATTER is aware, MATTER calls the music, MATTER does the thinking.*

Maybe, maybe not, I haven't made up my matter about this yet, but matter does the loving. No doubts, no doubts. Carnal certitude, clear and distinct sense data: in my flesh shall I see God. I came to love Adam when he was alive, totally chastely but with my body all the same. (In a different, milder way it was the same with Stella.) My heart beat just that little bit quicker every time I saw him, every time I heard him: my body-clock running fast. His presence warmed me, physically, like sunshine on my skin. Now and again my innards joined the reception committee too: lurched when I came across him unexpectedly; dipped when I *was* expecting him and he wasn't there. I was fascinated by the things he said, most of them, when I got onto his wavelength and could understand them, but if it had been someone else uttering them instead of him would they have fascinated me the same way? Of course not. Or if I had heard them always through a closed door and I had never seen Adam on the other side? Of course not, they would have shocked me out of my shoes. I was fascinated by them because they were Adam's, and I loved Adam because he was Adam, because he smelt nice, like hot hay, and moved like a high jumper, all springs and dithers, and hunched himself up like a gargoyle when he was still, and because his hair had a kind of downy golden border all the way round the scalp where it met skin, and because . . .

And because I hated him once he was dead. Before the fall, after the fall – he'd have had fun with that one. Adam's was not my first corpse, naturally. Old Father M. had seen to that. He was keen we should familiarise ourselves with mortality and was busier than Charon ferrying us postulants around the countryside to visit deathbeds. But his was my first known corpse, my first friendly corpse, my first personalised one.

I shall never forget my feeling of utter, utter revulsion. Rage, loss, helplessness – as if the swindle of the century had been pulled on me. Adam had gone, and all my love with him, and I was left looking at this . . . this lump of ill-arranged flesh, this shattered dummy, this mortician's attempt at jam roll. If, as I must hope against hope, I've lost God for good and He me, then I reckon it was there that we split ways: there in the Seminary Chapel, in the Eternal City in the heart of Christendom, while I stood inhaling pine deodorant and looking on the wreck of what only a couple of hours earlier had been, to my mind – to my matter – one of His Omnipotence's prize creations.

Suicide is a dirty word in religious circles, much dirtier than any I could muster (and I must practise if I want to fit into the secular world), perhaps the dirtiest there is, so nobody spoke it. None the less it was there, wafting around with the airwick. I sat by the coffin for hours, till my legs cramped, and practically everyone who came in made a point of repeating, almost like a litany, the official version. Accident, accident, slipped and fell, must have gone up on the roof to look at the night sky through the telescope and lost his footing, no other explanation, that telescope should be removed, it was a bad idea in the first place, not everyone trains it heavenwards either. And under all the repetitions, like a subtitle, ran: suicide, suicide, nervous break-down, loss of vocation, loss of faith. In some cases (and I would rack my brains later on, trying to remember which) you could read another – line sharper, more caustic: That's what comes of flirting with free thinkers, that's what comes of intellectual pride; you should have stuck with Aquinas, my boy.

I fancied I could hear an echo of it in the Rector's farewell prayer over the open coffin too. And I fancied he wanted it to be heard, even by Adam's father who had flown in that morning for the funeral. A fat father – a lawyer, no family resemblance for me to latch onto there. Perhaps especially by Adam's father. You never knew, these Scots.

Our dear young brother in Christ, so gifted, so brilliant. Let us pray that his agitated soul may find peace. The keener the mind, the more perilous the territory it has to tread. Highlands of rationalism. Lowlands of scepticism. (I glanced at Adam's father to see how he felt about this tacky topography but his jowly face stayed set.) The knife-edge ridge between inquiry and doubt. God tests His favourites with stringent tests. Amen and RIP and (another hidden subtitle, but one I had no quarrel with after my long watch) let's get this over with and shut the lid, please, quick.

I'm not sure I had a quarrel with the suicide thesis either. Not then. Not before the other things happened that set me thinking. It was true, Adam had indeed been dangerous places. Humeland, Nietzscheland, Jamesonia, Foucaultia, and not just quick bus tours of the main sites but long stop-offs in every village, every outpost. For one who championed short cuts he'd done a lot of slogging. Later, of course, I would learn his routes in greater detail, but even then, from the things he let fall in his Ben baiting, I knew he'd been around. *The soul is the prison of the body, Bendix*, no secret where that came from. *God is dead*, neither. Not quite so sure where he found the tail he used to add to it: *Yup, but he won't lie down: with every mortal blow, in steps the Geist and props the cadaver up again.* Nor can I trace this one, *re* the natural/artificial distinction, nor can I quite second it either: *Oil spill is just as natural as birdshit.* Maybe these were his own. Maybe he didn't believe in them himself, maybe he said them to dispel them and have a bit of a laugh at me on the way. But the

25

thing was, tourist or fact-finder, he'd visited these arid landscapes of doubt in his head, where men are just bones, and values dry up and roll like tumbleweed. He'd seen them and been affected by them. Even Jesus was changed by His days in the waste.

*   *   *

So, no, I didn't baulk at the official explanation, didn't question. Might never have questioned had it not been for that night – when was it? – four, five days later . . .

Wait, hold it, Ben. If it's clarity you're after then you're getting ahead of yourself. Chronology is vital. Adam died on a freezing February 3rd, 2001, lay in the chapel with an electric bell in his hand for all of the 4th and was buried on the 5th. He died after supper and was found immediately, owing to the noise and the fact that one of the washers-up in the kitchen was outside tipping away the rubbish, not ten metres distant from where he landed. There-fore February 2nd is the last entry in my diary for quite some while. For the next few days I was too churned up to write, and then the moment I started settling down again, or might have done, the second thing happened, and then the third and so forth, and that settled it. Instead of writing I had to read. To read, to piece together, to think and to decipher. Luckily, as far as my studies went, I had Adam's notes to guide me, a thread that I kept tight in my hand as I chomped and spat and chomped and spat, and ran past all the alley openings saying firmly to myself, cul-de-sac, cul-de-sac, not even bothering to stop and see for myself if they were, or if in fact they led somewhere instead. I had other things on my mind. Sometimes, when I was really pushed for time, I simply cribbed: put down Adam's opinions slap on the page, wholemeal and undigested as they were. I was afraid to begin with this might get me into bother – when I was called on to defend them, for example, without even knowing properly what I'd written – but strange to say it never did. Perhaps, because they came from me, little boring Benedetto, Don Anselmo never bothered to read them.

Later on, when I realised the risk I had run, I was simply afraid.

The final entries for end of January, start of February are, with one exception, dull as dust and I don't want to read them. Two earlier entries, though, I must put down here because they're important from the time perspective – in calculating when things started and when Adam got the first whiff of rat, and the rat the first whiff of his pursuer. And in rebutting the other theories, which I can't accept and shan't.

First my Greg dream, which is undated, but I reckon must belong to October, as I still call Adam the Scottie.

Have just woken after the weirdest dream. I dreamed I was standing in the square in front of the Greg with a group of tourists in tow. I was the guide but I hadn't learnt my spiel at all. Everyone was waiting for me to speak, and stomping and fiddling and getting impatient with me, and one woman, rather like my mum to look at, had started unfurling her umbrella and opening and shutting it at me the way you would to shoo off a stray dog. (Don't know whether it's significant, but besides my mum, the woman also looked alarmingly like the lady psychiatrist who interviewed me in London for my admission to the priesthood, and who to my enduring shame I lied to, on James's advice, when she asked if I was a virgin. 'Not? Oh, what a relief, splendid, then you're in.') The whole situation was getting more and more awkward, so eventually, close to panic, I went up to this tramp who was crouching on the ground at the entrance of the building and asked him if he would step in for me and do the explaining.

Forty thousand lire, he said, quick as a flash. I couldn't work out if this was cheap or expensive, but I said, OK, go ahead, vadi avanti, and gave him the money. (And I was ashamed because I knew I ought to stop first and do my arithmetic, and I knew I'd got the verb wrong too: it's vada with an a.) So he rose up, his garments flapping like a scarecrow's, and launched straight away into a kind of prophetic, soap-box declaration, full of warnings and innuendoes and general battiness. 'This place,' his voice rang out, 'is not what it seems. Oh nay, oh nay. The outside looks firm enough, but inside the building is crumbling like a cheese. Worms have eaten the lining between the outside and the inside – all that's left is two thin layers of paint. You think it's a university? Sham again. It's got University written on the façade, but if you step inside you will see all the tricks-in-trade of the Whore of Babylon's dressing table: her wigs, her war paint, her false teeth, her corsets, her stick-on eyelashes, her . . .' And then followed all sorts of objects that I didn't even know I knew about. Unless I saw them in the hospital when Mum was having her op.

The list was, yes, so way out and kinky that my subconscious must have jogged me into awareness, because the next thing I knew I was awake and listening to a real voice (at least I think it was a real voice, but it might still have been part of the dream) which was coming from close by – the Scottie's room, or else the corridor just outside. I couldn't hear much of what it was saying, only the up-and-down rhythms of peevishness and a curious little coda after a door snapped shut and the speaker presumably departed. 'Bright young devils go elsewhere,' was what it said. Bright young devils go elsewhere.

Query: What must it feel like to be a bright young devil instead of a rather dull young seminarist?

Sometimes, I must say, I am disarmingly honest – perhaps this will save me if ever it comes to the crunch. (Except, no, I was forgetting, there is no crunch, and I am already beyond salvation.) A further query rises in my mind today: how come my subconscious is so much wilier than I am? How come it spotted so early on that there was something seriously amiss in the seminary, while I saw nothing, nothing? No answer to that one. And now for the other entry: more noises in the night.

November 1st, 2000

Saturday. No lectures, Deo gratias. Air warm and very soporific. Think I shall give workout a miss. Or perhaps do just a few push-ups on the floor before supper, here in my room.

Should be studying but my head is splitting open like a pomegranate. (Saw a pomegranate yesterday, a real one, with a real split in its rind, in the Campo dei Fiori market. Weird object for a member of the veggie realm; it gave me the most unvegetarian thoughts.) There are six of us first-year students now that Phil has arrived: Mark One, Mark Twain, Phil, Kevin, Inigo and me, and all of us are in despair except for Phil, who is nearly forty and says, Unwind Lads, and, Cool it, with the crisis in vocations no one's going to fail to get a degree unless they fluff it utterly. It's not as if we were in the Middle Ages with all the MIT boys of the day scrambling for a church career; it's only us ambleshanks. And this is only Rome anyway, famous ecclesiastical backwater.

Hope he's right. (Though he can't be right about Rome surely? I was under the impression it ruled. Had quite a row over this the other day with Adam, when he said he'd been sent here as a punishment. I thought he was just being his paradoxical self and showing off. Maybe he wasn't and maybe California's the place after all. Like it is for prunes.) For my seminar I've sort of promised Don Anselmo I'll go for Hegel and the Phenomenology of Geist - a piece of intellectual bravado that, what with the set courses and the optionals, and a fifteen-page paper to churn out in my moth-eaten Italian before April 20th, I shall probably regret.

Sat up swotting last night till two. One of the reasons I stuck it so long was that I always like to wait till Adam's used the bathroom first - I'm sort of more comfortable that way, especially when I'm under the shower. Usually his all clear knock comes about midnight, but last night the work mood seemed to have gripped him by the lugholes, so in the end I gave up and dashed in for a quick polish with the flannel and then out again. When I gave my signal he didn't even acknowledge it. He was there all right: I could hear him clicking away at the computer; hissing at it and egging it on like a slow-moving donkey. (Why is it, when computers are so fast, that their users lose patience so easily? Next year, when I'm allotted one of my own, I dare say I shall hassle it just the same.) He was evidently too taken up by what he was doing to hear. He can concentrate like no one I've ever known.

As a matter of fact, not to boast, but I got quite dug into my studies afterwards myself. I'm re-reading Kafka's Metamorphosis at the moment - just to get my German going again - and, wow, I'd forgotten what a hold it gets over you. One minute I was in my tidy modern bedsit, listening to Adam's Internet bleepings filtering through the bathroom, and the next I was in that stuffy over-furnished mittel-European flat of Gregor's with all the doors and antechambers and sofas and cooking odours and worse. And by the time I got to the bit describing how Gregor used to prop up his huge beetle body against the jamb in order to listen in on the family's evening conversation I was so immersed in the text that, in retrospect at any rate, I could hardly distinguish any more between the real world and the page world. I felt so sorry for him. Imagine having to eavesdrop on your own father and mother in order to gain news of them. Imagine being closed off from them entirely, shut out of their lives, cast from them like the vermin you are. Imagine, too, the weariness of dragging around that stinking, festering carapace with the rotting apple studded into its hinge. It doesn't bear thinking about. Particularly not the moment when the poor giant insect drops off, exhausted by the effort of standing upright, and his head thuds against the door, bringing the speakers on the other side to an immediate, horror-struck silence.

And yet a few moments later I did have to think about it, because as I came out of my reading I had a distinct impression that I had actually heard a thud, just like Gregor's in the story, coming from Adam's side of the wall. And not only a thud but a scraping noise as well and a wild sort of chattering. Maybe an argument. 'What's he up to now?' Gregor's father wonders out loud, harsh and exasperated, not really wanting to know at all. (Climbing the walls? Hanging from the ceiling on his sticky pads? Slurping smelly cheese?) I don't have any feelings of revulsion towards Adam, if anything rather the opposite –

I find him what you would call in German 'anziehend'* - but it's not the first time I've heard funny noises coming from his direction late at night and I do start to ask myself much the same baffled question. What's he up to now?

He stirs something inside me, the bright young devil. I bet that was him all right, the bright young devil - there aren't many more round here fit that description.

* Note that I am unable to come clean out and use the English word attractive. I have to use the German word instead. As if it made any difference. *Anziehend, mein Fuss.* I was hooked already.

AND I WAS AFRAID

The owl of Minerva only flies at dusk. (Meaning you only ever see things clearly after they've happened. And *I* can't even do that.)

Yes, Grossvater Hegel, but when she flies she spurs you into thinking there were all sorts of things you could have seen or should have. Imagine if that night, or one of the other noisy nights, I'd put my eye to the bathroom keyhole and managed to see who it was Adam was arguing with.

It might have changed everything. I might have asked Adam more questions, he might have given me more answers, he might have come to trust me better, I might have watched over him closer, we might even have paired up and hunted as a team. Fear, bewilderment, loneliness, sheer hard work – at worst these would have been divided up between us and at best, well, at best they would have been eliminated altogether. Barring a little edginess under the shower, I don't think I could have ever felt fear knowing Adam was around, and as for loneliness . . .

Oh, shove the hypotheticals. What miserable things they are. I wonder if animals have them or if their alleged contentment springs from just that: the fact they're spared the ifs and if-onlys that skewer us humans through like kebabs? (Wonder too if Adam would pass that human/animal divide or whether he would treat it the way he did the natural/artificial one: *What grrrounds have you, Monkey Mug, for sealing yourself off in a separate compartment?*) It's useless to hark back, useless to recriminate. The noises; the restlessness; that picture of him in my mind, perched on the table in my room, all tensed and listening. Listening for what? For what? *I could break your priestly heart.* The things that happened – well, maybe they didn't *have* to happen the way they did, but they happened and there's no way now of unhappening them. Full stop, exclamation mark, desolation mark or what you will.

I miss him so badly. I only had him in my life for three and three-quarter months, if that, and now they're trying to take those away from me too. McShrink and his brand of orthodoxy; the Church authorities and theirs. Both brands run off me like water. Give me Hell, give me Oblivion any day; I don't want Heaven if Adam's not there.

Adamo, 1st pers. sing., pres. tense of the verb *adamare*, transitive. 1st conjug. – to love deeply or to fall in love. And so we come to the very last bit I need include: my pathetic night of fire. A cousin of mine has a little son who bursts into tears whenever people laugh at him and tries to cover it up by laughing with them. His mother, on the twee side, calls it cryfing. Well, twee or not, that's the effect this entry has on me: it makes me cryf.

Rome, January 29th, 2001. 2.30 a.m.

At last something novel to record, if only of a dead private nature. Woke up an hour ago and haven't been able to sleep since. Adam was here, in my bedroom. At least I think he was. No, I'm sure he was: I heard a funny, sharp little noise, like a piece of material being torn, which must have been what woke me, and when I opened my eyes, there he was, fully dressed, standing by the open cupboard with a pair of trousers in his hands, still hanging on the hanger. My trousers.

I couldn't move for the emotion, although I don't know what emotion it was, merely that it wasn't fright or anything resembling it. My heart, my lungs, my whole body crashed and I lay there still as a bag of cement. I wanted desperately to breathe - loud enough so that Adam could hear I was breathing and be reassured by it, because he looked a bit on the crashed side too, in fact the swaying of the trousers on the hanger was the only perceptible movement in the whole room - but I couldn't. I simply couldn't. And the longer the state lasted, the more the emotion mounted, because I knew that in the end I would snort like a geyser, and then Adam would know that I was awake, and that I'd seen him. And then he might be embarrassed, and I didn't want to see him embarrassed or in any way at a disadvantage because it would spoil my image of him somehow. But neither did I want him to be unembarrassed and in full command as this would spoil my image too, although in a different way.

In the end it was OK since what came out was more of a snore than a snort, and with this Adam unfroze, and I watched, still mystified, still quivering with whatever the emotion was, as he replaced the trousers in the cupboard, closed the door with the utmost care (care? Or was it tenderness? Or regret? Or . . . what?) and crept off again through the bathroom.

What can he have been up to? What can he have wanted? It's funny, but there seems to be no acceptable answer to these questions, or none that I can express in language. Apart, that is, from 'more Meltonian shoe polish'. If he wanted me - in whatever way - I can't admire him for it or be glad of it, but at the same time, if he didn't want me, then that doesn't gladden me either. Oh, how I wish I hadn't seen him. And yet that's not true, it can't be, because every time I conjure up the scene (perhaps a little fainter with each conjuring? No, if anything, stronger) the nameless emotion washes over me

37

*again like a wave, and I surf and somersault and tumble
and wait for it to ebb. And then miss it when it's gone.*

*Lord God, how have You made me? What recipe did You
use? Puppy dogs' tails or sugar? Or both, and in what
proportions? If the first, then where does Fanny fit in?
(Fanny Ardant, Lord, the actress. Yes, I know it's an odd
name, but she's French.) Adam says no knowledge is ever
to be shied from. He said that in the refectory last week,
loud, when the Rector was talking about genetic
modification, but I can't say I've got the guts to agree with
him. Not entirely. Surely some things, if there's nothing you
can do about them and no good they could possibly lead
to, are best left veiled?*

*   *   *

The night I did look through the keyhole I saw blank all of course,
but that was because it was dark.

And because I was shaking like a maraca in the hands of a –
well, whoever it is that skakes it. A Mexican, I guess. I've been
shit, shit scared more times than I can count since the start of this
business and with reason (good, the way that double shit tripped
out; making headway at last with the up-dating of my vocabu-
lary), but never did my fear anything like approach what it was
on that first occasion. When there was no reason at all, or no
reason connected with reason.

What woke me? The actual fright itself: it was there before I
even regained consciousness. I must have heard the trill, the
unmistakable little electronic overture, of the computer while I
was still sleeping, and the implications of what it meant must
have formed in my still-dreaming mind. A ghost? No, worse,
more like a zombie. Adam, but Adam as he was now, in his
irreversible patchwork state, stitched together as if by Professor

Frankenstein himself. I did my best to censor it but from my private store of horrors arose a nightmare picture of him, sitting there, crouched, griffon-like, over the computer, tapping on the keys with waxen bluish fingers that fell off him as he tapped.

It's terrible to awake to a fully installed fear, you hardly know what's got hold of you. I remember lying there, prickling all over with ice-cold sweat, and listening and listening with stretched-out ears, trying to gain control of my body, trying to breathe and not to cry out or do anything daft. And above all trying to kick into action the reasoning part of my brain which seemed to have gone AWOL. Clickety-click. Tippity-tappity-tip. There was someone there. Beyond doubt. Someone in Adam's room, fiddling with Adam's computer, and that someone was – *Get a grip on yourself, Benito, how can it possibly be me?* – OK, neither Adam himself, who I'd seen bricked into a hole a few days back, nor a computer-literate corpse or ghost – his or anyone else's – but a live, flesh-and-blood person of an enquiring, not to say prying, nature. What was he doing, this snooper? Hands off Adam's files. Hands off his notes and jottings and researches and whatever else private was in there. Here comes Cerberus.

In chihuahua version. As soon as I'd summoned enough control to stand without wobbling I got out of bed, opened the door and crept across the bathroom, one tiny step at a time, till I reached the door to Adam's room, and there, after several fumbling attempts, worse than Nelson with his spyglass, I managed to line up my eye with the keyhole.

Not, as I said, that it served much purpose. Barring a slight glow from the illuminated screen, cut to a tiny sickle by the key that took up almost all the space, I saw nothing. But I heard all right. I heard the tapping, then I heard it stop, then I heard a long silence as if the tapper was listening to see if he could hear me listening (it established a horrific kind of contact between us), and then, fortunately, I heard more tapping, followed by a sort of impatient whiffling noise – pff, pff, pff – and then came the closing fanfare as the computer was switched off and the unmistakable muffled bumpy noises of someone (large? Old? Both? Or neither, just clumsy?) getting up and leaving the room as quietly as possible.

It's lucky, I suppose, that I never mentioned this to anyone the day after. I longed to but I was stopped by . . . I don't know. I don't know what it was that stopped me: perhaps fear that my own fear would seep out in the telling. Ghosts, after all, don't have a very respectable ontological status for Catholic theologians, not unless they're Holy Ghosts. Zombies even less so. In particular I longed to tell Phil and to hear his nice flat practical townie voice telling me to belt up and that it was none of my business, that probably the Rector had given orders to someone to suss out the suicide angle and make sure there was no embarrassing material on Adam's files, nothing the police could latch onto if the inquest went ahead, or that could be fed to anti-clerical journalists. They loved that sort of thing. God Is Dead, Writes Seminarist in Secret Journal, and Plunges to Death from Roof of Luxury College.

No, it's lucky I kept my mouth shut and my fears to myself.

Because the noises went on, the next night and the next, and inside myself, in my panicky irrational part that McShrink says is my lead horse, I went on being shamefully afraid. Who was it who was in there, cut off from me by a breeze-block wall and a slither of bathroom? What was he doing? If he was still at the computer he'd be – what? Two, three metres away. But if, like me, he was sitting in the bed alcove he could be as close as half a metre. Fifty flipping centimetres. Maybe even less. What on earth was he up to? Why did he come back and back like this, night after night? Why was he taking so long over his task? Was he really a person? Or was he . . . ? Help, off I went. And another hole would open in my imagination and out would crawl another of my resident monsters, and another and another, besides whom the griffon and the zombie were winsome teddy bears.

When, on the third morning, I decided to put an end to this idiocy – in daytime I could label it that – by slipping into Adam's room myself, opening the computer and consulting the rubric of recent documents to see what the night prowler was after, it was already too late. The computer was no longer there. Someone, maybe the night visitor himself, had removed it.

DG, *Deo gratias*. (Though not for taking the rest, Lord. Not for the empty room, the missing clothes, the missing sneakers, the missing smell of hay. Did You love him Yourself? Was that it? It'd better be. It's about the only reason I could forgive You for, for taking him away: because You are a jealous God and wanted him with You in Heaven. Anything else and we're through. But then we're through already, no?) That day – a Wednesday I think it was – I started to relax a bit. I went to the Greg, sat through some lectures, took some notes, some of which made semi-sense at a later reading. I think it was also the day I chose my new confessor, Father Daniel Brooks from Philadelphia, first encountered beside me on a plastic floormat in the gym, our heads down, feet in the air, which is probably as bad an angle as any to judge people from.

In the evening I played ping-pong with Inigo, took a bashing, watched a totally immoral quiz show on the telly, with people being awarded hundreds of millions of lire for answering questions like, 'North, South, East, what's the missing fourth?' And then went bedwards, fairly calm, fairly unworried. The computer story, whatever it had been about, was over.

At three in the morning I was wide awake with terror. The noises had started up again, and this time they were coming from the bathroom. Not computer noises, evidently, seeing as the computer had vanished, but little tappings and scrabblings, as if a large rodent had got into my lav by mistake and was trying to get out again. Or a ferret ferreting.

I once spent a night with a bat. A summer night, a hot night, and I spent it under the covers, pouring with sweat, and didn't poke my nose out until well after daybreak, and then only gingerly. That night I did the same.

My diary, as I said, doesn't start up again for a while, so I can't calculate exactly how long the scrabbling business went on for, but go on it did, several more nights, not consecutive as far as I remember but off and on, which was sort of worse, and by the end of it I was getting paranoid. Too ashamed to mention it to anyone, and at the same time too proud. In the sense that I was protective of Adam's reputation. The aura of suicide was strong enough as it was, I didn't want rumours going round that reinforced it. They're searching his room. They're looking for a suicide note. They think he might have written a farewell letter to someone on his e-mail. They think he was in contact with some dangerous Rhineland Rebels. They think this, they think that – goodness knows what other dotty stories it might have generated: the students, apart from Phil, were a terrible bunch of gossips.

Then, just when I was on the point of cracking and turning to – I hadn't quite made up my mind about this; I was undecided between Phil and my nice new confessor Father Brooks – *Finis*. Silence. The noises stopped.

And there, had it not been for Chance, or Destiny, or God, or the Devil, or whoever sits at the pot and does the stirring, everything else might have stopped too, only it didn't.

IN THE SWEAT OF THY BROW

The Mafia have a neat way of killing off informers: they '*in-capretta*' them. Meaning they kid them, because a *capretta* is a kid, only it's not our idea of kidding. They truss them up with knees and arms bent backwards and the rope round the throat, so that every effort on the victim's part to free himself leads to a tightening of the rope and final self-strangulation.

That is my position now, I am *incaprettato*. If I turn to God I can only find damnation, if I turn away from Him my only refuge is madness. Either way, and through any move to escape, I am lost. McShrink doesn't understand, but how could he, hard-core Freudian that he is? Perhaps I should have chosen a Catholic analyst: she or he would have understood all right. But there again, how could I? What self-respecting, God-respecting Catholic would have taken me on? Oh, Adam, I know you didn't mean to, but what a terrible heritage you left me. My only link with you was one that drew me straight into the Cloaca Maxima – the big, big cesspit of all time.

How did I find it, the memento? Why, when I wasn't looking for it? Let me see if I can remember. Slightly pongy shoes, I think that was it. My workout trainers were getting a bit fruity, and I only had the one pair, so I washed them: popped them in the machine in the basement where we all do our light laundry and then brought them back upstairs to dry.

I didn't want to put them directly on the radiator as Mum says it's bad for the leather bits, and not having money of your own and always having to ask whenever you need new clothes makes you careful with your gear. They were pretty cool, too, my trainers – birthday present, lightweight, hi-tech, I was rather proud of them. But I wanted them dry quick. So I rustled around a bit, trying to think up a system, and eventually, in the back of the cupboard where my clothes hung, I discovered a ledge, just broad enough to hold the shoes, under which the heating pipes ran. Perfect, I thought to my unwitting self. Just the place.

So I put the trainers there. The ledge was a bit narrow, though, and one of the shoes immediately fell off, so I knelt down inside the cupboard to retrieve it and pop it back up again. And as I did so, not standing up, but reaching upwards from my kneeling position, I saw something that in the normal way of things I never would, or should, have seen: the underside of the shelf, on which was taped with black electrician's tape a little, flat, square parcel. Three floppy discs, wrapped up in a plastic cover.

Who knocked that shoe off? Who did I say were the putative pot-stirrers? Fate? God? Chance? Beelzebub? *I* knocked it off. *I* knocked it off, and *I* looked up, and *I* unstuck the discs, and *I* kept them. It's no good looking round for cosmic scapegoats, no matter what high-sounding names they go by, *I* did all these things, and the last one, which is the only one that really counts, I did knowingly, deliberately. Without deliberation – I didn't need to think for a second – but deliberately all the same.

It's funny, I should by rights have felt pique, disappointment: the finding, after all, poured a huge bucket of water over my night of fire, leaving just a soggy puddle. What had Adam been doing in my room that night I awoke to find him there? None of the hazy trouser-connected things I hoped or feared and that set me in such a twist about him: he loves me, he loves me not, he wants me, he wants me not. He'd been hiding the discs, that's all. Tearing tape, sticking the discs in place, and putting my clothes back in the cupboard from where he had removed them.

But, you know, I didn't feel disappointed in the slightest. On the contrary I felt chuffed and thrilled and buoyant because not only did his image return to its former Galahad purity in my mind but I had something of his to hold on to at last, something intimate, important and concrete. And, in a way, I felt that he had entrusted it to me: there were plenty of other places he could have left the discs but no, he had chosen me, Ben Gunn, to mount guard over his treasure. I could almost hear him saying it – he'd have been bound to have called me that under the circumstances, *Ben Gunn*.

It was, yes, a link, a secret thread that tied me to him, tighter than I had ever been when he was alive. (When, let's face it, I was little more than a favoured groupie.) And it was a thread that someone else was trying to catch hold of too. Because I had no doubt in my mind that this little square parcel was what the night visitor had been after. It all fell into place – the clickings, the scrabblings – first go for the computer, then, when you draw a blank, suss around for discs.

Why? What was so important about these discs? Well I wouldn't know for sure till I'd posted them into a computer and seen what they contained, but I imagined, as I had imagined Phil imagining, that it was all tied up with the inquest and with covering up any residual traces of Adam's suicide. Priests and police in Italy had a fairly pally, back-scratching relationship, it seemed to me; things had been cushy so far for the College, there'd been no boots stomping about the corridors, no material confiscated, no probes, no nothing. But I suppose if anything definite should have turned up, and got into the wrong person's hands, then, pally or not, the law would have had to take its course. Which would have meant things going public, the Press getting involved, etc.

That's more or less what I thought. Were mine the wrong hands? No, they were absolutely the right ones, and if I hadn't felt this I would have passed on my find to someone else straight-away. (To the Rector, I suppose. Without a thought about the state of *his* hands.) I never really bothered to answer this question at the time, though, because I never really stopped to ask it. I had the discs and Adam wanted me to have them – more than he did anyone else, anyway – and I was going to keep them. And goodnight to the dustbin, as the Romans say.

The next step was to read them. For a while I would just sit on them like a clutch of eggs, I decided, and savour my possessions, and then, when I got a chance of having the computer room to myself – no one peering over my shoulder or playing mine-sweeper at my elbow or making distracting remarks – I would read them.

Where would I keep them in the meantime?

Ah, that gave me my first cunning idea. (And I felt both proud and ashamed of it, like a child when it discovers it can lie without adults knowing.) I wouldn't keep them. I would make copies, and then I would put the originals back exactly where I had found them. Just in case. You never knew with Scots maybe, but you never knew with priests either, not these ones.

*   *   *

Bingo. Bullseye. I never noticed any signs of anyone rummaging around in my room, not even a clothes hanger out of place, and I'm hyper-tidy and was on the lookout all the time, but less than a week later the original discs had vanished from their hiding place.

It gave me the shivers when I discovered they had gone.

The other ones, the copies, sat in the computer room amongst hundreds of their brethren, each with a discouraging label: PATRISTIC HERMENEUTICS/In-depth readings 1, 2 & 3. Where do you hide a cross? asks Father Brown. In a forest of crosses. Where do you hide a disc? In a welter of discs.

I had opened the first one briefly and noticed to my surprise it contained a whole section of files, all labelled FAT. FAT 1, FAT 2, FAT 3 and so on up to FAT 18. There was other stuff as well, but I was interrupted and only the FATs stuck in my memory.

I chewed this over (*Och, Benglish, what a terrible way you have with words*) as I awaited my opportunity for an in-depth reading of the in-depth readings. It couldn't be weight problems as Adam was as thin as Kafka. And it couldn't be anorexia as, quite the opposite of Stella in this respect, he ate masses and wasn't that sort of person anyway – no fads, no fuss, no hang-ups. No, most likely it was an acronym. Federation of Australian

Trappists, that sort of thing. Or else an abbreviation. The dictionary, when I skimmed through it, suggested to me Fatalism, Fatiha and Fatwa but I tended to think it was simply Father – letters to his dad. In which case I would probably have to pass them on to the lawyer dad in person, but I reckoned that could be done without much trouble: I could just say I came across them, and it would be true.

Anyway. Whichever. I was in no hurry. Most people would be bursting with curiosity to find out what the night ferret had been after, and in a way I was too. But at the same time I clung tight to this moment of knowing but not knowing, having but not having. Was I afraid of what I might find? That too perhaps. I had another dream round about then, which I don't like to describe in detail, but it had to do with Adam, and with me barging into his room without knocking and finding him . . . well, in a very private moment, and him being furious with me and calling me all sorts of names, none of which began with Ben. McShrink likes to put another slant on it, trust him, but I think it was symbolic of the intrusion I was about to make, uninvited, into Adam's thoughts.

I suppose I'm a systematic person really. A plodder. As I'm always having to remind my mum, if I want to get anywhere I have to work at it, a bit at a time. I set aside two evenings a week – the Friday and the Sunday, when people were busy at their devotions and the computer room was emptier – and read my way in numerical order through all of Adam's files, starting with the FATs.

I was walking into a labyrinth from which I would not emerge until months later and only then with the greatest difficulty, dizzy as a dervish. They were Adam's files, you see, Adam's notes, Adam's reminders. Strictly *ad usum Adami*. He had never intended them to be found by someone else, let alone interpreted, he had simply bundled together the things that had seemed important to him as he went about his quest. It was like – it's hard to find a parallel – like coming across a map to an unknown country, plotted on unknown co-ordinates with the use of unknown symbols. Even today I have doubts sometimes about the route I followed and the destination I wound up at, which is partly why I am setting out my course again here, step by laborious step.

Courage, earwigo, once more into the maze:

FAT was for Fatima, for a start. Adam had been collecting material on the apparitions of Our Lady of Fatima, with particular focus on the Third Secret, made public to the world on June 26th, 2000.

Weird. Fatima is uncool among church intellectuals of today – one of those things that Father Simon would unhesitatingly scrape into the feeding bowl of the UF, the Unquestioning Faithful, and leave them to it. But then, he has a point: visions do pose a bit of a problem to theologians in this post-Freudian age, particularly children's visions, and as such tend to get pushed under the dogmatic carpet pretty quick. Great boost to the faith if handled right with the media, great quantity of egg on the papal face if not. I don't like to sound cynical or irreverent but what the subject conjures up in my mind is that scene from Fellini's film *La Dolce Vita*, with the two baby seers running around giggling, followed by a huge crowd of onlookers, hanging on their every word. 'There She is!' 'No, there She is!' 'Over here!' 'Over there!' 'By the tree!' 'By the cave!' Titter, titter, titter, and everyone, bishops and cardinals included, wheels round and follows like a flock of sheep. But to be honest I didn't know that much about the Fatima story myself – which just goes to show how low profile it has become – and had to mug up on it before reading any further.

The main facts were as follows. In 1917, in the little town of Fatima in Portugal, three shepherd children claimed to have seen the Madonna on six separate occasions and to have been entrusted by her with three terrible secrets of grave import to all mankind. The fuss and press coverage, even for those days, was enormous, and the Vatican muscled in quickly, although with hindsight perhaps not quickly enough: the first two secrets were already in the public domain and had been given a decidedly right-wing interpretation by the Portuguese bishops on the spot. These secrets contained a vision of Hell, and of the sufferings awaiting the world if its inhabitants continued on their sinful course: wars, bloodshed, violence, famine, and the persecution of the faithful, all to be heralded in by 'a night illuminated by an unknown light'. For these woes Russia was chiefly to blame – hardly surprising considering the date. Russia, according to the prophecy and/or the bishops' interpretation thereof, had been chosen by God as His 'instrument of chastisement' with which to punish an ever more wicked world. The only way of avoiding such punishment lay in a public act of consecration of what was termed, in cheerfully ante-PC parlance, 'that poor nation' to the Immaculate Heart of Mary on behalf of the Pope and all his bishops. If this request was not granted, went the final passage of the prophecy, then Russia would spread its errors throughout the world, raising up wars and persecutions against the Church. The good would be martyred, the Holy Father would suffer greatly and various nations would be annihilated. However, as the closing part of the Virgin's message stated, apparently verbatim, 'In the end My Immaculate Heart will triumph. The Holy Father will consecrate Russia to Me, and it will be converted, and the world will be granted a spell of peace. Portugal will always conserve the dogma of the faith, etc.'

So much for the first two secrets. The third, the one that Adam seemed to be most concerned with – and everyone else, for that matter – was kept under wraps for decades, accruing mystery like moss around a stone. Meanwhile the two younger children died in infancy in the post-war flu epidemic, and the eldest, Lucia, or Sister Lucy as she is now called, entered a convent, where she lives to this day in poverty, chastity and total obedience to the clerical powers that be, now aged well over ninety. In 1938 a particularly bright and extended aurora borealis – 'a night illuminated by an unknown light' – was taken by many as a vindication of the prophecy, and the mystery grew and so did the clamour. Six years later, in 1944, Sister Lucy, by then the sole repository of the secret, fell seriously ill and was urged by her superiors to write the secret down to prevent it being lost in the case of her death. This she duly did, with much agonising over the process, and passed the written message on to her bishop, the Bishop of Leiria, in a sealed envelope, giving the mystery mongers a tangible object to concentrate on. What was in this envelope that was so terrible it couldn't be revealed? When was it going to be opened? Who was going to have charge of it in the interim? Why didn't the Pope speak out about it? Why all the waiting?

This last question is still being asked today, although in a rather different tone: disappointed rather than curious. In 1957 Sister Lucy's message was passed to the Vatican for safe-keeping. Each Pope thereafter was reported to have peeped into the envelope, taken one look and blanched: unpublishable, unpublishable, and stuffed the thing back in its little wooden container with a shudder. A time-bomb ticking away in the papal apartments. And so the build-up continued until finally, in June 2000, John Paul II put an end to the suspense by rendering the message public, proving it to be, in most people's opinion, not a bomb but a squib, and rather a damp one at that. (So damp, in fact, that there were those who said it must have been deliberately dampened. We'll come to this in a minute.) More wars, more violence, more suffering for the faithful, more headaches for the papacy . . . Nothing nice under the sun, but nothing new either.

I don't know whether he had Fellini's film in mind too, but Cardinal Ratzinger, when he gave the Vatican's official theological comment on the text of the Third Secret the morning it was made public, certainly did an incredibly dextrous balancing act to try to keep everyone happy, from the simplest of the UFs to the cutting edge of the Catholic intelligentsia. His speech was stored in one of the documents on Adam's files: in it you could see the drop and the delicacy of the wire, and the wob-wob-wobblings of the poor Cardinal as he crossed the chasm with the first slat of the bridge in his hand. The shepherd children had been granted revelations, yes, he admitted, but *private* revelations. Visions, too, but *interior* ones, perceived with the '*internal* senses'. (*Whatever they may be, Benighted. And wherever they may be located; in the ruddy pineal gland, I wouldna' mind betting.*)

And yet this was part of the stuff that Adam had been collecting and that he'd gone to such pains to hide from the file ferret. Why had he been collecting it? And why had the file ferret been after it? At this stage it was impossible to tell. Altogether the assembled texts ran to about sixty-five pages. Most of these were either letters or articles from newspapers and journals, and most of them – the ones Adam found interesting, or at least the ones he had picked out in green type and/or underlined – seemed to have been downloaded from the website of some ultra-conservative rogue religious association based in South America, called the Fatima Falange.

Fatima Falange. Fatima Fanatics, Fatima Fantastication, if you ask me. Pruned out from among a host of lesser gripes about girl acolytes and Vatican Ostpolitik and the loss of Latin and how the Church is generally going to the dogs and fast, here is the Falange's main thesis, as it emerged from Adam's markings. I haven't changed anything, I've merely put things in a bit of order:

From the monthly journal <u>Fatima Falange Forum</u>, July 2000.

■ The purpose of this article is to prove beyond doubt that there are (or <u>were</u>, for our fear is that one of them has since been lost or destroyed) <u>two original manuscripts</u> written by Sister Lucy on the Third Secret and that <u>both documents were made available to the Church hierarchy</u>.

(Slightly wonky proof was then given in support of this thesis of the two MSS, but Adam skipped it and so shall I. It hinges on the fact that earlier witnesses maintained that the Secret was written in twenty-five lines on a single sheet of paper and contained the Blessed Virgin's own words, whereas the published version was in sixty-two lines, on four sheets of paper and contained none of Our Lady's words, only the seer Sister Lucy's. Convincing? Not up to me to decide, but the FFF was evidently convinced and that is presumably what mattered.)

Website interview, July 6th, 2000, with 'world famous Fatimologist' Dr Emmanuel Hackett of Peru.

■ Q: According to Cardinal Ottaviani, speaking in 1955, the Fatima message definitely <u>contained a prophecy</u>. Can you tell us, Dr Hackett, where the prophecy in the published message lies?
■ A: I can, willingly. It lies nowhere. The message of Fatima as revealed to the world by the Vatican in June contains a vision, not a prophecy. The two things are very different.
■ Q: Cardinal Ratzinger resolves this problem by redefining the word 'prophecy' as something very close to a vision. Would you disagree with the Cardinal on this point?
■ A: No disrespect intended, but the Cardinal is talking through his Cardinal's hat. 'Prophecy', as the word is commonly used, means a prediction of future events. And that, I believe, is what the Blessed Virgin sent us via the shepherd children of Fatima: a dire prediction about one or more future events, of concern to the whole of mankind. The worrying fact is, that for reasons unknown to us, this <u>message has not yet reached us, or not in its entirety</u>. Look, it's simple: although urged to do so by her Bishop, Sister Lucy hesitated for months before writing the message down, so horrible were its contents; until now, no Pope would publish it or

54

comment on it, and one of them, we are told, was
reluctant even to read it. Forty years of waiting
and Vatican humming and hawing and trembling on the
brink, and now out comes this. A vague vision of
sufferings for the Church ahead. (Or maybe even
behind, because the present Pope seems to think the
vision may well refer to his assassination escape of
1981.) Ordinary people however are not convinced:
they know there's more to it than that. Witness the
telltale 'etc.' at the end of the Second Secret. Are
we seriously to believe that Our Lady can find no
better way to wind up her message to humanity than
with an etc. like a secretary? No, it's clear that
the real text is either lost or hidden and the
Vatican is fobbing us off with a watered-down
substitute.

F. F. Forum, August 2000.

■ When Pope John XXIII read the Third Secret with
the aid of a Portuguese translator, his words were:
'This does not concern the years of my pontificate.'
In 1967 his successor Pope Paul VI made a pilgrimage
to Fatima but declined to speak privately with
Sister Lucy. His words to her, strikingly similar:
'You see, it is not the time.' How is it that both
pontiffs could be so sure on this head? The answer is
simple, they could be sure because the document they
had read, and which we shall henceforward refer to
as Document 1, contained a date, a specific mention
of a point in time, whereas Document 2, released by
the Vatican, contained none.

Dates, prophecies, Vatican manoeuvrings, suppressed messages – what was Adam doing collecting this stuff and storing

it on his files? If I'd found girlie pornography I think I'd have been less surprised. He with his hard, analytical Scottish nut – it was unbelievable.

There was worse to come. The second disc took ages to plough through but it paid off in the end for cribbing purposes – it contained mostly study material. Essays Adam had written, lectures he'd attended, notes he had taken of them and from his reading, philosophical musings and so forth. Quite gristly stuff, trust Adam, quite hard to get your teeth into. But then I didn't always bother: my teeth were more anxious to close on something personal that would throw a light on the suicide angle, so for most of the time I used Adam's own technique and munched selectively through the study notes in search of quips, asides, comments – anything that could reveal to me his mood at the time of writing.

But my teeth mainly closed on air. Self-expression was not Adam's forte, not even when he was writing by himself and for himself. All I came across of a remotely personal character was the following. First a couplet,

```
Nature and Nature's laws were hid in night;
God said, Let Newton be, and all was light.
```

tailed by a parody couplet,

```
Nature and Nature's laws were bathed in light;
Chance said, Let Darwin be, and all was night.
```

that quite honestly I found a bit depressing. Next a jingle, to be sung to the tune of 'Speedy Gonzales', up-beat in mood but so disrespectful that I hardly like to reproduce it. Its opening line, just to give the idea, ran, 'You betta wake up Parkinson Paulie', and its overall message was that the Catholic Church urgently needed to overhaul its moral theory in order to survive much longer as a world religion. Away with arrogant little jumped-up Man as the self-styled centre of the universe, and in with Life itself

56

in all its forms: ecological balance, birth control, animal rights, etc. – all of Adam's favourite hobby horses corralled into a jaunty, mocking rhyme.

And thirdly an extremely childish (for Adam) spoof of the creed, which ran as follows:

```
'I believe in one God, almighty Father, creator of
heaven and earth, and of all things visible and
invisible . . .' I believe these words to be a
comforting jingle, wrought by man's fear and man's
imagination. I believe too that the same holds true
for all supernatural or metaphysical discourse,
right across the board . . .
```

After this came Adam's blacklist of the various discourses, and very black it was too. But no blacker than many other things he'd said to me with a dollop of irony and his lopsided, hitched-up smile that took out the sting. I'm sorry I didn't erase some of the worst stuff before putting the discs back in place, however, because without the smile you could draw much graver conclusions about the author and his set of beliefs.

Such as, Bencher? Such as . . . Oh, I could list several, but if I am to fall at this stage into the trap of questioning Adam's vocation and his presence in the seminary, then I am virtually handing myself over to the Furies without a fight. That's the enemy's thesis. Let the enemy consider it, not me. Let's also see what he makes of Adam's brief closing line:

```
No creator made the universe but, who knows, one day
the universe may throw up a creator. Then we may see
some sparks. Divine ones.
```

Let him stuff that down his ever-whiffling windpipe and let him choke on it. I *know* Adam was smiling when he wrote it. I know he was.

Anyway, that's the gist, the flavour, of the *journal intime*. Adam was still findable there, his voice still encoded somewhere, somehow, in the binary language of the discs. Much more foreign to my mind and much more mystifying was the next batch of documents, the MILLs, concerning the millennium.

Again I give only a tiny sample, with the original stress marks unchanged. There were ruddy dozens of the things:

■ Ludwig Heinrich -- 17th C. As soon as the millennium touches its end, there will rain from the sky a pestilence never before seen on earth. And the pestilence will drain all force from man; and man will no longer have the power to fight, not even against <u>the worm that crawls on earth</u>.

■ Anon. Russian staretz -- *c*. 1850. The last century of the millennium is a mountain on which three beasts sleep. The first one will wake up in the beginning of the road. The second will wake up in the middle of the road. And from its throat will come fire. <u>The third will wake up at the end of the road. And from its throat will come horrible heresy</u>.

■ Anon. Templar prophecy -- no date. Near the middle of the last year the signals and <u>the number</u> will appear in the sky. Iron birds will obscure the sun. <u>The beasts of the Apocalypse</u> will come out of the sea and the flames from Hell will surround the earth.

Tosh, codswallop to someone of Adam's intellectual sophistication. I could hardly believe it was there and I was reading it. What *was* he up to? Compiling a treatise on superstition? He hadn't even consulted scholarly founts like Boehme or Goerres or Rosenroth or whoever the up-market millennial boys are (and perhaps there aren't any), he had simply downloaded these reams of ill-digested blather from what I call the Internet shite sites. (Hey, more excreta, another spontaneous motion. How come I have so little trouble with the S-word, when the B-word and the F-word still floor me? McShrink would have an answer to that: he'd say it's because I'm stuck in a pre-genital phase, and I think he'd be right, I am, like an overgrown elf with too much body hair. Who do I fall for? Other elves like myself. No, not like myself: far prettier, far more elegant. Fanny Ardant has elfin blood, and so does her distressing double; Adam was pure elf; and Stella was elf, too, of sorts, under the grungy crust. Was? Probably still is, but I'd rather not think of that: Stella dead, Stella alive – both alternatives just freeze my heart.)

Number, Beast, Worm: whatever the rationale was behind this hairy collection of crackpotteries, it evidently had something to do with the coming of the Antichrist – the heinously evil arch-enemy of Christ, who, according to Revelation and other sources, will lure mankind to the brink of damnation, before finally throwing in the sponge to Our Lord Himself on the Day of Judgement. When I moved on to the third disc, in fact, I discovered, amongst other things, a batch of documents, numbered one to ten, all entitled SPOILER, which is one of the names attributed to this shady gent (or lady, not to be sexist):

The Spoiler
The Man of Sin
The Beast
The Little Horn
The Prince that shall Come
The Idol Shepherd
The Angel of the Bottomless Pit
The Crooked Serpent

Yahushuah to his friends. I like these names; they have a certain grandeur about them. As too do the quotes. But with this third group of files there is of course a shift in literary quality as Adam moves into the heart of Apocalypse literature proper – the Holy Scriptures – and adds the third element to his heady cocktail, giving us, in my own summing-up:

The theory of a
STILL UNREVEALED FATIMA MESSAGE

containing:
A DIRE PROPHECY FOR THE NEW MILLENNIUM

concerning the coming of:
ANTICHRIST, aka THE SPOILER, etc., etc.

heralded and followed by:
A SERIES OF CATACLYSMIC EVENTS

Bang in the middle of *Omen* territory. Fine, for those who like it. But what was Adam doing there? Did he believe in these things? From what he said and read and wrote, there was no real telling – he juggled words around like ninepins. You had to look at his actions to read him right: he had consecrated himself to God, therefore he believed in God and in the priesthood. He uttered blood-curdling, soul-shattering opinions but he did good deeds, constantly, pretty well exclusively, therefore he believed in good-ness and in spreading it through the world. Ergo he believed in evil also. But *this* kind of evil? Numbers and signs and portents and monsters and a ten-horned beast coming out of the bottom-less pit on D-Day and dragging us all to our doom?

Father M. used to have a good line when people asked him about this wilder-shore prophecy stuff and mass-miracles and stigmata and whatnot. Leave those things to Hollywood, he used to say, God is not in show business.

If He is, Ben Hur, He has a lousy scriptwriter.

*   *   *

60

Here I was, then, thrashing around in this jungle of quotations, trying to find a footprint, a thread, a trail of crumbs – anything that would lead me in a definite direction instead of just blundering around at random. The path looks simple now I've done the machete work, but I promise you, it was a long, hard slog.

I had to be stealthy about it too: look around me all the time when I was at the computer, to make sure nobody was noticing what I was up to; cover up my electronic tracks so nobody would see the weird names of some of Adam's files cropping up on their screen afterwards; SPOILER, WHORE, ECLIPSE, 666.

And all the while I was engaged in a parallel search for the file ferret, about whom I had no information whatsoever, except that he was possibly old and possibly large and possibly clumsy and possibly wandering around in exactly the same jungle I was, working his way through Adam's files in search of . . . whatever it was he was after. Or possibly not because just possibly his task had simply been to get rid of the stuff, Amen.

It's funny. Even on such a wide-toothed description you'd think I'd have been able to exclude *some* members of the community, say half a dozen or so at the least. But the extraordinary thing was, I couldn't. Not all of us were old, of course, and not all of us were large, in fact there were some tiddlies amongst us – not to be heightist, but the Vice-Rector Father Julian was a borderline Danny de Vito (without, obviously, a smattering of the charm). However, when I started looking closely I noticed that there was not one single person who you could say was properly in charge of his body. Not the way athletes are, for example, nor the way Adam was either. Even Mark Twain, our best sportsman and, DG, recent victor over Inigo in the ping-pong stakes, was a bit gangly: he spilt salt at table, tripped over his laces, goofy things like that.

Priests enter the priesthood for many reasons, and many of them praiseworthy, but one of them, which is woven so tight into the others it is not always separable, is because somewhere along the line there has been a matter/mind breakdown in communications.

A matter/mind split, Adam would probably call it: you can't have communication unless you've got two discrete things to begin with, still less a breakdown. Well, then, a matter/mind split. I don't know about the Antichrist's branding process on the foreheads or the hands of his adepts, or wherever it is he's supposed to print his logo, but judging from personal observation, Christ definitely marks out his clergy in some analogous way: psyche, snip, soma. Forty-two people, all of them maladroit, all of them priests, would-be or actual. You can't have just a chance assembly of forty-two maladroit priests. Can you?

You can anything. I tried next to use the time criterion – rule out my five companion tadpoles on the grounds they literally hadn't had time to get into whatever it was Adam was into. But strictly speaking, strictly using, this criterion didn't work either. The priesthood is a network: its members can be clannish. The newcomers were unlikely to be after Adam's files on their own accounts, granted, but any one of them, even Phil, could be working on commission for some superior. Make use of Tiddleypush, Rector dear, if there's any little job needs doing. We have found him most obliging here and know he would be delighted to be of help. Yrs in Christ, Signature.

No one to exclude means no one to trust. And no one to trust means no pals, no muckers. I, who am such a sociable person by nature, began to be looked on as a loner. An aloofer. A loner, what was worse, mourning over an unpopular rebel who had exited in a tactless, tasteless way, under a cloud that still cast its shadow over the whole establishment. Had I been brilliant like Adam himself was, I could have been dubbed eccentric and excused. There would have been a slot to put me in. But I wasn't brilliant: I was average and so was my performance as a student. Friendly yet isolated, hard-working yet with so little to show for it; result: a contradictory creature escaping classification and creating a little mobile moat of perplexity that surrounded him wherever he went.

Don Anselmo was disappointed and showed it by contracting his mono-brow, every time he saw me, into the shape of a huge furry caterpillar on the move. If he'd had political designs for me it had been on the strength of my affability, my capacity for making friends. And my parroty linguistic abilities maybe – Pieces of eight, *Pezzi da otto*, *Achtelstueckchen* and so on. But now both skills were on a definite wane. My 70,000 lire-an-hour Italian lessons were called off smartly, and Signora Marcozzi with her brassy hair and Sergio Tacchini teeth went on to coach a different, more responsive and rewarding pupil, viz, the upwardly mobile and upwardly puffed Inigo. (Such a pain in the butt, he did wonders for my anti-racist agonising: you can't be unspontaneous in the way you relate to a pain in the butt.)

Onigo, Inigo, rather you than me. I needed my low-profile for my puzzle-work. There were the SPOILERs still to comb through thoroughly, and then there was WHORE, ECLIPSE, RESTRAINER, FP AND MEMO. I'd done a quick scan through MEMO already, but it appeared to contain nothing of interest. A few little odd phrases – bit short, bit cryptic – and a row of telephone numbers, one a doctor's by the look of it.

I had also opened the file entitled 666 early on, because the title struck me, and I wondered why its contents had been entered separately and not just classed together with the SPOILERs, but it was empty save for the unhelpful words, written in tiny type, `You can say that again, buddy`. It also had a far more recent date than the other files and was a Microsoft original, like MEMO, whereas all the others were modified HTMLs. But what did that mean? Something? Nothing? Who could say?

The SPOILERs proper on the other hand looked as if they might prove a bit more fruitful:

- `Little children, it is the last time:` <u>`and as ye have heard that antichrist shall come`</u> `. . .` (John, 1st Epistle 2.18)

- `And in his estate shall stand up` <u>`a vile person`</u> `. . .` (Daniel 11.21)

■ And in the latter time of their kingdom, when the transgressors are come to the full, <u>a king of fierce countenance, and understanding dark sentences, shall stand up</u>. And his power shall be mighty, but not by his own power: and he shall destroy wonderfully, and shall prosper, and practise, and shall destroy the mighty and the holy people. (Daniel 8.23, 24)

OK, OK, so far the burden of the song was clear: he's on his way, the Beastie, and he's going to wreak havoc. Subtly at first, through manoeuvrings and blandishments and bribes, he will worm himself into a position of absolute political power, and then he will strike. Phase one will be the elimination of the notion of good from men's hearts – a kind of universal moral brainwashing – and phase two the physical elimination of all those who still manage to resist him after the wash. How shall we recognise him? Well, I whinge about my criteria for finding the file ferret but the ones I managed to assemble from the bulk of Adam's notes were not much better:

1) He will possibly be a Jew from the tribe of Dan, possibly a Syrian, possibly neither. See Genesis 49.17: 'Dan shall be a serpent by the way, an adder in the path, that biteth the horse heels, so that his rider shall fall backward.' He may have Italian citizenship though, as, according to some texts, he will either be a total reincarnation of the Emperor Nero or will be possessed by the selfsame (pretty competent!) devil.

2) Stronger than possibly, probably, his life will mirror that of Christ in various unspecified ways, from the Virgin Birth onwards. But the mirror will be black: i.e. for virgin read *demi-vièrge*, for ox and ass read wolf and snake, and on in this photo-negative key – all the bright bits dark, all the good bits bad.

3) Possibly also he will have extra-white teeth, sparkling eyes, pale eyelashes, wear clothes dunked in wine or vinegar, be given to tripping people up (see Genesis again above), have no taste for women, and `'tether his donkey's foal to the vine'`, whatever that means. Perhaps, updated, something to do with drug dealing? Tie to the vine = make someone addicted to an intoxicating substance, donkey's foal = the gullible young. (Oh, my God, the Camorra connection! I'd never thought of that: the Camorra's big in the drug-dealing business.)

All the above hypotheses, however, first formed in a systematic way by Hippolytus around AD 230, were marked in red in Adam's original notes, which I took to mean the opposite of green, i.e. dicey, uncertain. Green marks were reserved for the following two quotes only, both from Revelation:

■ And I saw one of his heads as it were wounded to death; and his deadly wound was healed; and all the world wondered after the beast.

(I don't wonder they wondered. The Evangelist also mentions that the beast will have seven heads, which *would* be a way to spot him and no mistake, but Adam didn't list this verse, he merely inferred from the above that the Antichrist will bear a head wound and undergo a near-death experience.)

■ Here is wisdom. Let him that hath understanding count the number of the beast: for it is the number of a man; and his number is Six hundred threescore and six.

(Wake up, Rabbi Ben Nahman: Gematria, not his mobile phone. The letter count for NERON CAESAR totals 666.)
Finally, after these ways of identifying the Antichrist, came the

recipes for getting rid of him, and these were not only picked out in green but put in large capital letters:

- And through his policy also he shall cause craft to prosper in his hand; and he shall magnify *himself* in his heart, and by peace shall destroy many: he shall also stand up against the Prince of princes; BUT HE <u>SHALL BE BROKEN WITHOUT HAND</u>. (Daniel 8.25)

- AND I WILL <u>CALL FOR A SWORD AGAINST HIM</u> throughout all my mountains, saith the Lord God (Ezekiel 38.21,22) . . . And I will plead against him with <u>PESTILENCE AND WITH BLOOD</u>.

- And I will turn thee back, and <u>PUT HOOKS INTO THY JAWS</u>. (Ezekiel 38.4)

Bit contradictory these methods, unless words and hooks are held in the foot. But it's no use my trying to joke about it all. It was no joke, it is no joke, it is ghastly, ghastly serious. Whichever way you look at it. And I look at it often, every way I can, and cryf my eyes out.

KNOWLEDGE OF
GOOD AND EVIL

By mid-April I had finished my sifting work but I still wasn't much the wiser. The file FP, standing for False Prophet, had yielded the information that the Antichrist, when he came, would be accompanied or preceded by precisely that: a False Prophet, an Anti-Baptist. OK, well that was part of the parallel lives business anyway: Jesus and John, Spoiler and Mate.

WHORE, for Whore of Babylon, was a quickie too because it contained only a short article with a couple of underlined quotations, again from Revelation:

■ And here is the mind which hath wisdom. The seven heads are <u>seven mountains, on which the woman sitteth</u>.

■ And <u>the woman which thou sawest is that great city</u>, which reigneth over the kings of the earth.

Which the author of the article – pretty raving article it was too: New Age baloney encompassing everything from Sphinxes to UFOs – took to mean that the birthplace or dwelling place of the Antichrist would be Rome. Seven Hills, Heart of Christendom, and right on our doorstep, *grazie tanto*.

RESTRAINER was a bit more complex, hinging as it did on a really knotty passage from Saint Paul's second epistle to the Thessalonians.

■ And now you know <u>what witholdeth</u> that he might be revealed in his time. For the mystery of iniquity doth already work: only <u>he who now letteth will let, until he be taken out of the way</u>.

Or in a more modern translation:

■ You know too what is <u>still holding him back</u> from
appearing before his appointed time. Rebellion is
at its work already, but in secret, and <u>the one who</u>
<u>is holding it back has first to be removed</u> before
the Rebel appears openly.

This was all mixed up with utterances of Our Lady, made during
her appearances at La Salette, Lourdes, Fatima, Garabandal and
Medjugorje. Great mishmash. Luckily the author of the piece,
another allegedly famous Fatimologist, Lourdologist, Garaban-
dologist etc., provided an interpretation. Of sorts.

In short, Saint Paul is saying that the Antichrist's
destiny cannot unfold until someone or something
described as the 'Restrainer' or the 'Withholder'
is gone.
  Who or what is this restraining power? Exegetes
have no doubt, it is none other than the Blessed
Virgin herself, the arch-enemy of Satan and our
traditional shield against his wiles. (Remember: 'I
will put enmity between thee and the woman,' 'And
the dragon was wroth with the woman,' etc.) If we
examine the messages Our Heavenly Mother has given
to us over the years we can see that in the battle of
Good against Evil she is actively engaged on the
side of her Son, attempting with all her might to
prevent, or at least postpone, the most terrible of
the serpent's attacks against humanity: the sending
of the Antichrist. Unfortunately, however, if the
text of the unrevealed Fatima message is what we
think and fear it is, Our Lady is warning us that
this power of hers, granted to her by God at the

moment of Jesus's birth, has a temporal duration of
two thousand years only, and is therefore <u>due to
expire as from Christmas Day of the new millennium</u>.

The last file, ECLIPSES, was simply a NASA list of eclipses of
the moon, on which the eclipse of January 9th, 2001 had been
marked out from the rest.

So there, at last, were my ingredients: 1) Fatima prophecy of
the Antichrist's arrival, to take place in Rome, in the new
millennium. (Was this where January 9th fitted in? Was it
perhaps his birthdate?) 2) Advice on how to spot him. 3) Advice
on how to get rid of him.

But it is one thing to be in possession of eggs and meat and veg
or whatever and another to have a ready meal. At present all I
had in the way of cuisine was Scottish stew. Hotchpotch. Hash-
your-own-haggis.

I'd been in the habit of talking to Adam regularly in my head as I
worked my way through his collection – loneliness, I suppose. But
the sad thing was that the more I progressed, and the more oddities I
came across, the harder it became for me to make contact with him.
His voice became increasingly muffled under the layers of farrago
until it wafted out at me like the rantings of the soapbox orator in my
dream: Hark ye, hark ye, the Antichrist will be born in Rome at the
start of the new millennium. I couldn't hear Adam uttering a phrase
like that except in jest. But jest doesn't run to all those megabytes.
Where was the Adam I knew? Where was the scoffer? Where was the
mind-boggler? Or had I never known him properly at all?

Maybe it was for this reason – a longing to get in touch with the
old Adam again – that I finally stopped poring over the other files
and shifted my attention to the small file labelled MEMO. The
one I had dismissed earlier as containing nothing of interest. Who
could say? Perhaps Adam had been working for someone else all
along? Perhaps the doctor was a sociologist and he had been
collecting data for him? Sorry, her. Something like that. Anyway
it was worth a try.

So I abandoned my jigsaw puzzle (missing only one or two key pieces, as I see now, close as that), went out to a tobacconist, where you can buy a whole lot of other things besides bus tickets, blew Aunt Cath's Easter pocket money on some call cards, and set about telephoning.

There were ten numbers listed on the file, two without names attached, and one name without a number, just a string of question marks:

```
06/3626663
06/6880117
Alessia . . . . . . . . . . . . . . .  06/4250093
Paolo (pal of G.) . . . . . . . . .  06/3395016
Alberto R. . . . . . . . . . . . . .03375059732
Paola Serra . . . . . . . . . . .  06/5839002
H.R. . . . . . . . . . . . . . . . .  06/8092024
Dr C. Muzzi . . . . . . . . . . . . . .06/55677
Sister John of God . . . . . . . . . .????????
Lulli . . . . . . . . . . . . . . . .  06/4927903
```

Above the list were written in Italian the names of two saints: Saint James and Saint John on the Island (whom I'd never heard of). Saint John on the Island was underlined: <u>San Giovanni all'Isola</u>. The other wasn't. Below the list were the following brief notes:

```
Are there nursing homes in centre? Check.
Urine/eyedrops/heart condition -- which?
Dante: eclipse = power vacuum? Check.
Date? Probably trad. but check.
```

And underneath them, in bigger, darker letters:

Check out Shorty

Finally, to close, in typical Adam style, there was a slightly altered quotation. From Blake, I've since discovered:

```
I give you the end of a golden string,
Only wind it into a ball:
It will lead you in at Hades' gate
Built in Jerusalem's wall.
```

Hades' gate. The mouth of Hell, and I was about to enter it.

*　　*　　*

It's hard ringing someone up when you don't know who they are or why you are ringing them. You're apt to blow your chances before you get started, so that by the time you've found out what questions to ask, the person on the other end of the line is no longer willing to answer them, having sized you up, quite correctly, as a telephone crasher. No encyclopedias, thank you, and down goes the receiver.

Telecom Italia runs a service of number identification but, besides costing me double, it was virtually useless. I entered the two nameless numbers but the recorded voice simply told me they didn't exist. So then I dialled them and discovered they *did* exist, but beyond that, nothing much else. The first one rang without answer for days, and when it finally did, a woman's voice just said, *Si?* I'd got so used to there being no answer that the monosyllable caught me short and I forgot all my carefully prepared questions and said, *Um* back, and then *Pronto*, and she said *Pronto, pronto*, who's that speaking? and I said, *Scusi*, who's *that* speaking? And she said crossly, You're the one who rung, who's THAT speaking? And I was so flummoxed I just rang off.

The second nameless number was answered by a man, who said in a dog-tired voice, *Laboratorio*. After my experience with the woman I reckoned that was already plenty and left it at that.

Urine, heart condition, nursing homes, a doctor, now a laboratory.

Paolo next, because there was no surname and it looked as if he
might be a friend of Adam's. Or let's say a friend of a friend,
going on the assumption that G was a friend.

Here I struck luckier. But not from the information point of
view. Paolo was Paolo Argenti, a research student at Rome
University, faculty of literature. Nice, helpful chap, from the
sound of him. He'd never met Adam, only spoken to him a couple
of times over the phone, didn't even know that he was dead, but
sounded fazed in a sympathetic way when I told him so. When
had it happened? Beginning of February? *Porca misera*, what a
sad business: he'd spoken to him not much earlier – when would
it have been? – middle of January or thereabouts. No, sorry, he
couldn't remember who it was who had brought them together.
G.? Didn't ring a bell. Knew lots of G.s. Probably a student, he
would ask around. Male or female? Never mind, he'd try both.
What was it Adam had wanted to know from him exactly? Hang
on a sec, let him think. Dante, that was it: well it would be Dante,
wouldn't it? Dante was his speciality. Adam had wanted to know
whether Dante had ever written about eclipses, and he had told
him, yes, he had, and had read out to him over the telephone the
passage from *Paradiso* where Saint Peter rails against the usurper
of his empty papal chair on earth. *Il luogo mio, il luogo mio che
vaca* – that bit, which is accompanied in the text by a description
of an eclipse of the sun. God hiding His face from mankind, so to
speak, letting evil take its course, the way He did during the clou
moment of the crucifixion. Adam had seemed to be satisfied with
this and had thanked him and asked in closing whether there was
anything on lunar eclipses as well, any verses where the metaphor
was used in the negative sense, to represent e.g. a hiatus in the
power of the Devil. He had told him there wasn't, not in Dante,
but that the Sun/Good Moon/Evil dichotomy was pretty standard
by then, traceable to Pythagoras and earlier, and that there were
almost certainly other instances in the literature of the period

where this use of the metaphor had been made. More thanks, and that was about it.

Ah, that accounted for the equation. Expanded on these lines, it now read: an eclipse in the firmament = a power vacuum in the Heavens/Depths. Covered sun, and God has his eyes shut; covered Moon, and it is the Devil who has shut his. Which in turn meant, or so I reckoned, that I'd been right, and that Adam, going on this wacky principle, had singled out, not the traditional December 25th but January 9th, 2001 as the birth date of the Antichrist. The restraining power of the Holy Virgin – well, I wasn't sure how he had squared that one: perhaps he had allowed for a fortnight's margin before the power faded completely. Or perhaps he'd decided that the Virgin thesis was wrong, and that the Restrainer was in fact the Devil himself, biding his time till the moment was ripe. (In which case the Antichrist, from a logical point of view, would have slipped into the world against the Devil's will, during an infernal power-cut, and this didn't quite tally.) But these were details I could work out later. The gist of Adam's reasoning was clear: something crucial had happened during the lunar eclipse to shift the power balance, and into the world had come Spoiler. OK. All I had to do now was to look around Rome for a seven-headed baby born that day, reeking of vinegar, and Bob's your uncle, I could turn him over to the Signatura.

Another limp joke that rings hollow as a cavern. It wasn't until I reached the last of Adam's numbers, though, that the dreadful seriousness of it all came home to me.

What did I glean from the others? Precious little at this stage. It would take cross-referencing on quite a busy scale before I got anything useful out of the list. For the present Alberto R. was a young, polite but baffled university student, name of Rossi, studying journalism, who had never had any contact with Adam or even heard of him. Dr C. Muzzi, the C standing for Carlo, was some kind of bigwig hospital guy, protected by a secretary I didn't seem able to dodge. Alessia was not a person but a computer firm that had helped Adam to install some software on a professional basis in September and October 2000; the name of the actual technician they had sent didn't show on their files, but they said they'd check on this and ring me back. H.R. was a voice on a voice-mail – female, American – telling me its owner, Helen Rosenfeld, was away. And Paola Serra was the working wife of a suspicious, baby-minding husband: she kept odd hours and seemed never to answer the phone herself, no matter when I rang.

Lulli? Well Lulli was the bolt from Heaven. Or from Hell. Lulli was not for cross-referencing, Lulli was best left in peace, poor Lulli. Lulli had answered questions enough. Lulli was the surname of a young couple, man and wife, who were going through a bad patch in life, so the wife told me, a tired note entering her voice the moment I mentioned Adam's name, on account of the fact they had recently lost their firstborn son, a baby just fifteen days old. Adam had been sent to them by the hospital to offer counselling. They hadn't wanted to see him to begin with – not being that religious, you understand, not really having much time for priests and prayers and what have you – but he'd insisted, and perhaps it had helped them a bit to speak to someone, in the end. They had been very upset when they had heard of his death, just couldn't take it in: another young life quenched. Death seemed to be dogging them nowadays. There are those times in life probably . . . Maybe things would look up one day, but just now . . . *un momento brutto*. Was I a priest too, like Adam? Had I been sent to replace him? Because, nothing personal, but she thought they'd rather manage on their own now, if I didn't mind.

How can you ask questions of a person like that? Insist? Bother them? Intrude on their grief? Adam had obviously used up most of the mileage on that front already. Besides, how can you ask questions at all when your head is spinning like a fan? Whhhhrrrrrrrrr. First I had to think. Link things together in my mind to form a picture. And I already knew the picture would be ugly as sin.

Where was your baby born? In which hospital? On what date?

Was it by any chance January 9th? How did he die? Did Adam tell you he was a priest, an ordained priest? Did he tell you that or did you just assume it? Was it he who told you he had been sent by the hospital? Did you speak to any other priests besides Adam? Who told you he was dead? All these things I could and should have asked but I just didn't have the heart, or the presence of mind. All I managed was the fourth, and it came out clumsily, pressingly, queering my pitch for future probes. I should have put it differently: asked when the monthly memorial of the baby's death occurred so that I could have Mass said for him, something sympathetic like that, but my Italian was hardly up to it, so instead I just blurted out, 'Signora Lulli, please tell me, was your son born on January 9th?' 'January 9th?' she repeated dully, a slight slur of – I think it was anger by this point – colouring her voice. 'Of course not. January 9th was the day he died.'

'I see. I'm sorry.' The words sounded stilted – the effect of shyness and of creeping paralysis as suspicions literally froze the thinking part of my mind. They were met by an equally stilted disclaimer on her part, '*Le pare*', and I could sense her steeling herself for outright discourtesy, should I continue on this track.

But I didn't because I didn't care to. Didn't dare to. I knew I would have to bother her again with more questions but later, when I'd figured out which ones needed asking the most urgently. If I could risk, say, three more questions, or perhaps only two, then I had to be sure they were the right three, or the right two. In the meantime I must just try to stay in her good graces. I said something about Adam and about my own sadness at having lost him, which put us back on a better footing, and on this note I think we closed. Exit, for the time being, meddlesome priestling number two.

No, I'm wrong, there was one more exchange between us. Just before hanging up Signora Lulli asked me my name – she was the first person on the list to do so – and I said quickly, 'James', which was the only other name that came into my head. I don't know how I managed to do this, when I'm so slow on the uptake and truth is such a habit to me, but I did, and I'm glad I did. I was James in all my investigations from then on – a tiny shred of cover, sorely needed.

Think, you nitwit James, get your thinking cap on. I stared at the mouthpiece of the public phone and then, hardly connecting at all, into the eyes of a waiting Filipino outside the booth. Backwards and forwards: mouthpiece, eyes, mouthpiece, eyes. Little black circles, bigger black circles, and inside me, tumult. January 9th minus fifteen days was December 25th. Christmas Day. The jigsaw pieces hung together more smoothly now: the baby had been *born* on Christmas Day 2000, the exact date on which the Virgin's power had been due to lapse, according to the Fatima Falangists, and had *died* on the day (at the hour? That was a question I must ask) of the following lunar eclipse, when presumably the Devil's power had been in abeyance and the new-born Antichrist, therefore, at his most vulnerable. Traditional birth date; death date as recommended in the files, if you had been following them closely and took seriously the theory of the power gap. I had been playing a game on a computer, tapping keys and juggling with words and solving, or trying to, an electronic puzzle. All clean and cerebral. And now suddenly there was a dead baby to contend with – a real baby, flesh and blood, and now decaying flesh and stagnant blood, poor little creature – bang in the centre of the screen. Adam had been asking questions of Signora Lulli, therefore Adam didn't know what the game was either. All along, like me, he had been following the tracks of someone else: piecing things together that he'd gathered . . . who knows where, who knows how, but definitely from another person's computer. It struck me that maybe not even the markings in the texts were his but had come to him ready-made, from the original downloader. Hence the difference between types of file: the Microsofts were Adam's and the HTMLs were not.

I should have been aware of this, should have thought of it earlier, it was so obvious. *Mea culpa*.

A family, a baby, a wild hypothesis built round this baby, and then acted on without mercy. A madman, therefore: a madman in our midst. Hospitals, laboratories, a doctor, a journalist, a Dante expert, a computer expert, too, most likely. Two saints, a nun (a sister, maybe a nurse?), a row of question marks. Adam had been grappling with this material, the way I was grappling with it now, and Adam had paid for his curiosity with his life.

I must have left the booth, or I think the Filipino would have knifed me, but I have no memory of doing so. Lucky I wasn't run over either as I must have crossed a few roads afterwards in a complete and utter trance. I needed to speak to someone so badly it hurt. Adam hadn't slipped and he hadn't committed suicide: Adam had cracked the riddle, or come so close it made no difference, and had been pushed off the roof for his pains.

A crazy conclusion, and I was crazy for drawing it.

But, no, it made gruesome sense. *I could break your priestly heart.* Well he almost had, I could hear it splitting. Adam had discovered something, something terrible, atrocious (like the planned, cold-blooded elimination of a child? Exactly), he had gone about combating the plan in his own way, and he had failed.

Adam was cleverer, far cleverer than I was, and braver too, and it hadn't helped him. The madman, the file ferret, the murderer – yes, murderer and now double murderer – had won hands down. What hope had I of winning against such an adversary when Adam himself had failed?

None, not the slightest. I was ignorant and bungling and alone. And scared out of what wits I had. I was a gonner before I'd even started. Best drop the whole thing and save my goose-pimpled skin.

Only how could I? How could I go on with my life, my studies, my formation as a priest, knowing or suspecting what I knew or suspected now? Don Anselmo: it could be him, for example, my own tutor. Or it could be the Rector, or Pascal, or Father Julian; it could be anyone. I could be studying for the priesthood under Adam's murderer, sitting down to meals beside him, talking to him, taking Communion from his blood-stained, sacrilegious hands.

No, no, no, I couldn't stay still and couldn't backtrack. I must either leave immediately – Rome, the seminary, the priesthood, everything – or else go on, no matter what, and get to the bottom of this horrendous affair. And then . . .

Oh, my God, dear God, what is this wheel You have tied me to?

. . . then we would see. Meanwhile I must take stock of my position. Keep a cool head, Ben, keep a cool head. Courage isn't necessarily a good thing, courage can make you careless: fear isn't necessarily bad, it keeps you on your toes. Uncomfortable, being on your toes all the time, but more uncomfortable still being bested by a maniac and killed. You have two advantages over Adam: one, you may know less than he did, but at least your opponent doesn't know that you know, and thus you are operating in the shade, in safety; two, you are angrier than Adam ever was or could have been, because Adam fought his battle on ethical grounds and you are fighting yours on personal: he wanted justice, you want revenge. And anger, so they say, is a potent antidote to fear. Let's hope they're right.

THE VOICE OF
MY BROTHER'S BLOOD

*What's that about justice, Benthamite? I WANT REVENGE
TOO. Get him, nail him, expose him. Do it for me. You say
you're angry, and you're still darned alive, imagine me, then,
dead as a doornail and not turned thirty. What's your gripe
against him? He deprived you of your fancy boy, that's all.
What's mine? He deprived me of my life. And what shall it profit
a man if he shall gain a million brownie points and suffer the loss
of his own life? Eh, Ben? Answer me that. Promise you'll avenge
me if you can, promise.*

I promise.

*Good man. It's all there, on the discs, everything you need to
know. More or less. Use your noddle for the rest; I know I used to
mock it, but that's just my way; it's not a bad noddle, it's quite a
good noddle as noddles go. Use it.*

*Saints and hospitals, for example: put the two together. It's the
same in England, no? Saint Thomas's, Saint Bartholomew's and
all those guys. No, forget Guy's, that'll only muddle you, stick
with the saints. Saint James, San Giacomo – a hospital, only it
wasn't that one, it wasn't quite central enough, it was the other:
San Giovanni all'Isola, all'Isola Tiberina – Saint John on the
Island, on the Island in the middle of the Tiber. That's why it's
underlined, see? Maternity ward. Got it? Maternity ward. Go
there, ask around. See if any people on my list work there.*

Off you go. Oh, yes, and, Benjamin Bunny . . .

Still patronising, but it was great to hear his voice again,
coming through clear.

Yes?

*Don't let Mr McGregor get you, the way he got me. I dubbed
him sick, sick, sick, and so he is, but that was an understatement:
he's a perilous criminal and he's fly as they come.*

Sick, sick, sick? Ah, six, six, six – You can say that again, buddy. I see, 666 – that's one file disposed of. How did he get you, Adam? I forgot to ask you that. How did he lure you up on to the roof? What stratagem did he use, and how did you fall for it?

I fell, all right, you can say that again, buddy, and in bigger print, but probably not for the stratagem. What do you think? Maybe I just went up there for a fag or a joint or something, or a sniff of your bootblack, and he caught me unawares. Doesn't really matter now. I was cocky, I let my guard slip, I underestimated him. Don't you do the same.

I'll try not to. It would have helped me a lot if you'd only given in your notes a clue as to his identity. But you didn't, did you?

Ah, sorry, a man can't think of everything. Perhaps I wasn't too sure myself, and perhaps that's how he got me: because I didn't recognise him in time. Or because he isn't a he but a they. Nibble on that one, Bunnyrab. Trust no one.

No one? No one at all? But I so badly need an outlet for all this angst. Could I write to James, do you think? Just sort of outline the facts to him in the vaguest of possible terms? Just . . . ?

No one means no one. Means no one, means no one.

*　　*　　*

Oh heavy cross, with no Simon of Cyrene to lay it on even for a stretch. If before I had felt alone in the community, now I felt isolated. A replicant, a martian, a member of a different species, and a threatened species at that. Everyone I looked at, everyone I spoke to – Pass the beans, Ben. Did you see the football match on telly? How's the essay going? When do you start your pastoral work? That'll keep you busy, all right – every single, apparently harmless and friendly face surrounding me bore the potential mark of Cain.

I built a picture in my head, like one of those painted scenes at the seaside with a hole in the middle, depicting the roof at night, with Adam sitting there defenceless on the wall by the telescope, and an evil black-clad figure creeping up on him with out-stretched hands, ready to push. Then I tried fitting various faces into the hole to see which looked the most convincing.

They all did, unfortunately, but for some reason my attention settled most heavily on Pascal – Father Blaise, our treasurer – whose bare, Van Eyck features and stick-out ears and shaven head seemed to lock in perfectly. Screwtape to the life. And Father Snooty Simon, his face clicked in well too, but that was probably just inverted snobbery on my part, since the face itself was innocent-looking and bland, like that of an old and rather world-weary baby.

Next I tried envisaging a computer scene, sitting my candidate down in front of a keyboard, but that didn't help much either: the clergy seem to have taken up computers *tutti con brio*, the way they took up quills and brushes in the Middle Ages. Perhaps Pascal and the Rector looked slightly more out of place than the rest, because they both had scribes to do their desk-work for them, but even they did the odd bit of tapping now and then. No, computer savvy was a useless criterion.

I shifted to the whiffling question. I was sure I had heard whiffling that night, as the ferret worked at the computer. Who whiffled as they ate? No one that I noticed. Certainly not Father Simon – far too well-mannered. Who were the asthmatics, then, who were the fatties, the puffers, who were the smokers? Old Father Hilderbrand had a heart condition, his breathing was short all right, but what came out was more of a wheeze than a whiffle: hee-ack not pff, pff, pff. Our mini Vice-Rector Father Julian – call me Julian, but treat me like Cardinal Giuliano – suffered from hay fever, but I tended to exclude him on size grounds: Adam would either have dragged him down with him or flipped him overboard in a trice. Michael smoked – toady Michael – he was one of the few. Phil smoked, Robert from second year smoked and a couple of older students as well. The Rector smoked a pipe, but only on Sundays and feast days.

Or was breathing nothing to do with it and should I be looking for the irritable and impatient instead? Wide field there.

And talking of wide fields, our catering was done by the Little Sisters of the Holy Raiment. ('Oly Raiment? I'll do me own mending, thanks, said Phil when informed of this.) Why hadn't I included any of them in the line-up? Was it sexist not to consider women as potential murderers? I supposed it was, although the voice I'd heard arguing in Adam's room had been male enough from the sound of it . . . But women, too, can have deepish voices, some of them, and some men squeakers. Oh dear, another of my dratted dilemmas. And another row of faces to fit into the hole. Sister John of God, the mystery lady who'd earned herself all the question marks, who was she? Where did she come into it? And *Shorty*? Who the fish was Shorty?

No, churning things round in my head wasn't going to get me anywhere, not any more. Adam was right, it was time to put my boots on and go and do some field work.

A TILLER OF THE GROUND

McShrink is full of explanatory theories for taming the untame-able, but then that's his job: schooling ghouls. 'I notice, Ben,' he says, 'that when you see and hear things a bit out of the ordinary you preface your account with, "I saw, at least I think I did, but it may still have been part of the dream . . . No, I'm sure I saw . . ." Or heard or whichever. You do this often. Has it ever occurred to you that you may have difficulty separating the real world from the world of your imagination? Just a suggestion.'

Has it occurred to me? Of course it has, midgewit. It's occurred to me the way a thrown lifebelt may 'occur' to a shipwrecked sailor and I've clung to it with the same fervour.

Only some things, though they may be nightmares all right, are not dreams. The hospital, for example, that was there, solid enough, parting the muddy waters of the river Tiber like the prow of a ship. Samuel Johnson would have stubbed his gouty old toe on it for a start. What with outbuildings and forecourt and gardens and whatnots it covered pretty well half the island. The island's not much bigger than a football pitch, but still . . .

And Paola Serra inside of it; she was real enough too. A stocky, cheerful, cardiganed bustlebody in her late thirties, with a greasy ponytail (rather ponyish all round to tell the truth, particularly the rear) and squat, dependable tootsies peeping through her white paramedic's sandals. Reality, normality, you can't ask a person to show much more evidence of either. Unreal, in the sense of unbelievable, unacceptable, inconceivable by a sane mind, was merely what she told me.

Perhaps it's lucky I caught Rosenfeld on the phone first, before going to the hospital, because it gave my questions a convir slant. If I'd been fey or vague I think Serra would have to me aside with her ponytail like a bothersome fly. A knew, if not what questions to ask, then at least along what lines to ask them.

How real Rosenfeld was, I'm not so sure; I only ever contacted her over the telephone, just three times in all, counting the voice-mail, but the voice sounded real enough when I finally caught up with her. Of all the people on the list she was perhaps the only one who had been in any way close to Adam: she was a friend, or so she claimed, had known him from university days, had acted in a play with him once. Brecht, she thought, or derived from, but couldn't quite remember. Adam had worn a toga – he looked good in a toga. She stopped in her tracks after she'd said this, as if thinking exactly what I was thinking, and said gruffly that she couldn't bear to think of him now. So I suppose she was a friend. Although it was hard to imagine what sort. I asked her why Adam had called her recently – if he *had* called her, that is – and she confirmed that he had, but then complicated matters by telling me that he quite often did, and she didn't therefore remember any particular occasion or reason over any other. Silly of me, seeing (or hearing) she was female, but I felt downright jealous. What was her profession? I asked. What was she doing in Rome?

She sounded a bit put out, as if I ought to have known without asking. She was a doctor, she said, she was the Embassy's number one recommended internist to all US citizens here.

Oh, was she? And then, dring, dring, went the bell in my head, and no more puzzle or jealousy. A doctor. Of course. Another doctor to add to the roster. Wait a minute, had Adam perhaps called her recently on a technical matter – something to do with babies, with newborn babies?

Hey, that was weird: what was I? Psychic, or had I bugged her phone? Yes, he had, now I mentioned it. But not so recently, quite a time ago, like around Christmas. Maybe earlier. He'd rung wanting to know – for some friend of his who was writing a crime story or something – how you'd fix it if you wanted to keep a little kid that was perfectly healthy in hospital. Or how she would. And she'd told him that, herself, she'd either simulate a heart condition by overheating the cradle with an electric blanket, or else she'd put some trouble-causing agent in the eyes with the eye drops that are applied at birth, or, better still, she'd swap urine samples and turn in a false specimen.

Heart condition, eye drops, urine. The three items on Adam's list. I was still loping along one step behind him as he loped along behind someone else, but at last I felt he and I were drawing level. He had suspected murder, right? So he had reasoned the baby was most likely born healthy but had been detained in the hospital under false pretences. Why? Well, obvious, even I could see that: because it was easier for the murderer to carry out his plan in a hospital, where the babies are kept in a crèche and people are coming and going all the time, than in a private home. Especially if the murderer was a priest. An unknown priest in a hospital corridor at night: Good evening, Father, and scarcely a glance; the same sight in the corridor at home, and you'd scream your head off. (Unless you lived in a seminary, like me. No, not like me, not like me at all, because these days a swirl of a soutane in the shadows, and I'm ready to scream too.) OK, OK, then, so that was why Adam had called up his doctor friend, H-for-Humility Rosenfeld: simply to find out, in theory, how such an end could be achieved. She had duly come up with three possibilities, he had noted them down, and then . . .

What had Adam done at this point? Exactly what I was doing now, I should imagine: i.e. he had boarded the island via the gangplank/bridge and made for the hospital in search of either Muzzi, Serra or Sister John of God, whichever of the three, if any, was to be found there, and had questioned them to discover which, if any, of the three hypotheses was the right one. (Make it be none, God. There is still time to call it all off. I haven't yet worked out the costs of this business to my nervous system, or my belief system either, but I have a feeling that if I go on living in a seminary where a homicidal lunatic is at large You may lose a postulant before long. Can You afford this, with the drop in vocations? Mull it over.)

Adam may or may not have known which person he was after.

I didn't, but although Muzzi was definitely a doctor of some kind and Sister John of God was increasingly likely to be a nurse, the rhythms of Paola Serra's timetable instinctively made me plump for her when I went to the desk to ask.

P = 33.333 per cent, Success rate = 100 per cent. *Ben trovato*, I heard Adam say as I made my way to Maternity. *Or Ben trovata, seeing she's a female. But don't foul it up now, will you, by being over-finicky with the truth. Remember: the lady probably still thinks I was a fully fledged priest, sent to bring Christian comfort to the poor Lulli family in their hour of need. Don't disabuse her. No need for you to lie, just rub your hands together and look priestly and let things take their course. If you play it right she'll either assume you're my successor, or else she'll think you've been sent on a delicate insider mission to discover whether my death was linked to my state of mind. You could ask her, for example, typical loaded questions like: Did Padre Adamo – yes, that was what she called me, and try not to laugh when you say it – did Padre Adamo ever seem to you unduly stressed or depressed by his counselling work? Was there any case in particular that seemed to upset/tax/obsess him? Go ahead, don't worry, she's a nice co-operative person, like the Dante bloke.*

She was a nice person, very nice. Practical, down to earth and sturdy – a pit pony amongst ponies. But we had a terrible, terrible talk together. After we'd finished I was so shaken I had to go into the church on the island and harangue a crucifix, like Don Camillo. She had liked Adam, she said; she had met him several times, always in connection with the Lulli case, on which Adam was doing a home follow-up. My vague allusion to, not suicide quite – I thought that would be overdoing it – but a stress-related death on his part, set her up in arms in his defence, and I warmed to her even more.

Although not she to me. Impossible, she said, giving me a disgusted look. Unthinkable: Padre Adamo was such a strong, decisive character, and so religious. In a deep way, she meant, not in the usual slippery churchy way at all. (Another look at me.) And so dedicated to his work, so patient. The Lullis – well, the

Lullis had staved him off to begin with, particularly the mother, who'd gone on a sort of silence strike after the baby's death and you couldn't blame her, but Padre Adamo had won her round. Got her to talk. He said talking was everything when you had a burden to carry – solace, distribution of weight, liberation even. And it was true. Because when she herself had told him . . .

'Told him what?'

My ears must have pricked up physically, terrier-style, because she stopped short and gave me another sharp look and said, 'Nothing', in a very guarded tone.

I reckoned I'd best ask the most important question first. Or the one I then thought of as the most important. 'How did the Lulli baby die, exactly? Could you tell me the whole story?'

She shrugged, not looking too enthusiastic, but picked up as she spoke. It was an SDS, she said, a Sudden Death Syndrome, a cot death. It had happened – no one was quite sure – probably some time after supper, when vigilance was a bit slacker, what with the mothers watching TV and the day-staff going off duty and handing over to the night. But it wasn't that sudden, not really. The baby had been ailing since birth. It had kidney trouble – there was something wrong with its kidneys. Something pretty bad, pretty serious, she didn't know the medical name. The girl, the mother, had always refused to accept that her baby was ill because it *looked* so healthy. And it was true, it did: *sembrava così sano*. So obviously she couldn't accept the death either. Hence all the legal fuss. But that's what tests were for, no? What hospitals and doctors were for, too, really: for helping you see what was wrong with a person underneath the surface.

Were they? Then what I needed was a madness test to run on all the members of the community. A litmus wafer in the shape of a host, for example, that turned blood red when it touched the tongue. It all fitted, everything she'd told me so far: kidneys, urine, seemingly healthy baby, mother's scepticism, sudden, all too sudden death; at just past supper time too, eclipse time, with the moon obscured and the Devil's power in check. God had turned deaf on me: it all fitted, in spite of me praying so hard for it not to. Wait, though, the legal fuss, what was that? The mother had said nothing to me over the phone about legal procedures. 'What legal fuss exactly?'

'Oh . . .' Impossible for a person like her to look shifty, but for a second Nurse Serra, or Orderly Serra or whatever her title was, looked slightly uncomfortable. Oh, nothing, she said. It was unlikely to go ahead. There were no grounds really. But the family was bringing a case, or trying to, on account of the . . . She looked down at her stubby toes, twiddled them, and then looked up again, straight at me. Oh, well, she might as well say it, it was no secret really. They'd been asked not to discuss it with outsiders, on account of the bad press hospitals were getting nowadays, but she'd told Padre Adamo after all, and I was a priest like him, and priests . . .

I took Adam's advice, cast my eyes down, rubbed my hands and murmured something indistinct (oh, forgive me, Lord, forgive me everything while You're about it) regarding the seal of confession and the generally trustworthy nature of the clergy – murderers, naturally, excepted.

It worked. 'On account of the hook,' she finished.

'The hook?' Something, I didn't know what, caused a little quiver inside my head, like a mouse nibbling at my brain.

The hook, yes. One of those fastener things. Teeny-wee. It had been found in the child's cot, pressing against its cheek. Matron had found it. The baby had been lying on it and it had made a little gash in his jaw. It had nothing to do with the death – it couldn't have done, everybody said that, because if the baby had choked on it, then it wouldn't have been lying where it was, it would have been in his throat. But the mother had made the most fearful rumpus – well, you would, wouldn't you? – and the Direttore Sanitario had come round and hauled everyone over the coals, and for a while it had looked as if the hospital might be in big trouble. But in the end it had all simmered down because, well, because the babies' clothes were always provided by the parents anyway, and the hospital layettes – those few they kept, for premature babies and such – were strictly fastener-free, and always had been. There just weren't any hooks or eyes or poppers or whatever in the whole department.

The nibbling went on but I couldn't attend to it now. Later; I'd search for the cause of it later. 'Couldn't it have dropped off someone's clothes?' I asked. 'An adult's?' And as I spoke I imagined the murderer, bending over the cot to do his terrible deed (how, though, if he couldn't use his hands? With his elbows, I suppose), and God himself, in punishment, loosening the hook from the fiend's clothing in order to make sure he didn't get away with it. I was still sold on Divine Justice.

'Much too small,' said Serra. 'Like I said, it was one of those little tiny ones – typical of old-fashioned baby clothes. Myself, I think Matron should have just kept quiet about it and thrown it away. It would have saved the mother a lot of upset. You know, when you think there's carelessness involved and that someone else is responsible . . . it doesn't help you come to terms with your loss.'

No, especially if you're right and someone else *was* responsible. And the other names on Adam's list? I must ask about those too, now I had the chance. 'Who is Dr Carlo Muzzi?' I tried. 'Have you ever heard of him? Does he work here?'

The ponytail swung sideways with too much momentum: Nurse Serra was evidently relieved to be let off the hook. (The hook. The hook. What *was* it about this hook?) 'I don't think so, no. No, no one of that name works here. Why?'

I would trace him later. Maybe he was the arch-villain, or one of them. 'No particular reason, I just wondered. What about Sister John of God? Ever heard of her?'

Different reaction, inasmuch as the ponytail bounced instead of swinging. Of course she had, she had worked there as a nurse. One of the contract nurses from the convent. A timid little mousy thing, very quiet, very reserved. From Bangladesh, or, no, maybe it wasn't, but it was somewhere beginning with a B. Padre Adamo had asked about her too, he was keen to get in contact with her about the Lulli business, but it was unlikely he had managed to because the nurse had left soon afterwards. Gone back to the convent, she supposed. These nursing orders, they were always shuffling their personnel around. It didn't help foster a good team spirit.

Could she remember the name of the Order? I reckoned she wouldn't be able to, if she couldn't remember the name of the country. In fact she couldn't, but she said not to worry, she'd soon find out. And with that she trotted off to the end of the corridor (cantered was more like it), disappeared through a doorway and came back almost immediately with the news that it was the Ordine di Santa Marta. Ordine Ospitaliero di Santa Marta. And she handed me a Rome telephone number on a slip of paper.

'If you do make contact with Suor Giovanna,' she said, 'well, that was what *we* called her – in Italy nuns don't have men's names as a rule – tell her she left her sandals in the changing room. At least I think they're hers.'

Sister John of God had left quickly, then. I guessed as much. Like a hired killer. Ship your she-jackal in, and when she's done her job, ship her out again. (Only what was the job in this case? To swap the urine samples? Yes, I figured that was it: to substitute bad urine for good and fake a kidney complaint, in order to make sure the baby was still in hospital for the night of the lunar eclipse.) It was all so coherent, and so unbearable it wrought havoc inside me, starting with my manners. I think I thanked Paola Serra properly for all her help, and took leave of her politely, out of habit but I honestly can't vouch for it (nor, looking back, do I much care): I was on automatic pilot again by then. Because at this point in our conversation the mouse in the archives of my brain gave a great big nip, and the relevant information bled suddenly into my consciousness, obscuring all else.

Ezekiel 38.4 – I will . . . put hooks into thy jaws.

It had been on Adam's files, highlighted and in capital letters. Methods for impeding the advance of the Antichrist: I will turn thee back and PUT HOOKS INTO THY JAWS.

IT IS NOT GOOD THAT
MAN SHOULD BE ALONE

The hook business really freaked me out. It was strange it should have such a strong effect on me. What was it, after all? Just a detail, just a little piece of metal, nothing in comparison to the murder of Adam or the murder of the child. And yet it somehow brought home to me the full horror of what I was involved in, in a way these larger events had failed to do. Perhaps I need things to be small in order to get my head round them, perhaps my head itself is small and that is why. I remember once seeing a documentary about the Holocaust, and it was the same with that: the mass atrocities – the charnel pits, the gas ovens, the streams of trampled humanity – all these passed me by like shadows from a past I felt hardly concerned me; and then suddenly there was this shot of a tired, bent old lady, sitting on an upturned crate, with a young Nazi standing over her with a whip in his hand, holding it under her chin, tilting the head back and forcing her to look straight into the camera. And it was that shot that did it for me, that single shot. It unlocked all the violence of the others; tore down my defences and left me reeling.

I had turned to God then, in an agony of bewilderment that He could allow such evil to enter His creation, and I turned to Him now, in the church on the island, for the same reason. Only this time He was that much harder to find. As can be seen from the minutes of our – one-sided? two-sided? real or imaginary? – conversation:

ME TO CRUCIFIX: I warned You, Lord, and You didn't listen. Or if You listened, You didn't see fit to pay heed. I honestly don't think I can go on this way much longer. You took Adam, You took this child. You stood by and let someone slay it and put a hook in its cheek in order to fulfil some crazy old prophecy, made by some crazy old geezer back in the year dot. OK, very minor outrages in this world of Yours where outrages abound, but outrages all the same.

A sparrow cannot fall without Your knowledge, so You reassure us. Well, it's CLUNK, CLUNK isn't it, all around the clock? And I'm not the least bit reassured. I'm dead rattled, if You want to know. I know others get around it all right but theodicy is my stumbling block.

Faith is faith and brain is brain and ne'er the twain shall mix. Kierkegaard was right, Cardinal Newman was right: we must either swallow a credo whole or utterly reject it. There is no such thing as theological knowledge. I can't *study* to be a priest, there is nothing to learn, nothing to study, there is only the whole Corpus of Belief to be downed in a single mouthful, chewing strictly forbidden. *Hoc est enim corpus meum* – take it or leave it. And I am ever more strongly tempted to leave it.

It is ebbing, Lord, my faith in You is ebbing, swirling away like water down a plughole. Hear me, see my plight and have mercy. I beg, I beg of You, do something, quick, to stop the flow.

ME FROM CRUCIFIX: I doubt it's worth saving, this faith of yours, Ben. One evil priest – no, not even, just the shadow of one evil priest, flitting around in some dark corner of your mind, and you stand to loose every drop? It wasn't faith at all, then, it was arrogance. Who are you, to tell me how to run my world?

ME TO CRUCIFIX: No one special, Lord. One of Your middling creatures. Sorry, I am frightened and alone, and the stress is telling on me. I am cracking up. You cracked up just a little, too, didn't You, that night, in the garden? You can understand.

ME FROM CRUCIFIX, OR MAYBE CRUCIFIX TO ME: Poor little blighter, that's better. Of course I understand, not for nothing did I don human form. Man isn't made to bear a lot of weight alone. It's your arrogance, again, makes you think you can tackle this business single-handed. Tell you what, instead of whingeing to a dead Scot or a piece of wood, go and find a real, live person whom you trust and respect, and talk to them about it. What's that? Adam says not to? That'd be the dead Scot, no? Well, make up your mind, who or what do you choose to believe: dead Scot, piece of wood, your own conceited voice or the voice of your true Saviour? Get along with you. Oh, and Ben, just one last thing. Don't worry about your little Scottish sparrow. I caught him all right in the end, you know. I'm a good fielder.

*   *   *

Whose voice was it I eventually obeyed? I don't know, I don't know whether it was God's or mine or whose it was, let's say Necessity's and leave it at that. I had no choice, I had to speak to someone, I was coming apart at the seams. So off I went to my confessor to bare my poor shivering soul.

Dr Macpherson, my present confessor and hence in a way Father Daniel's replacement, doesn't often show much interest in the factual side of things. He doesn't ask me, for example, how I discovered who Dr Carlo Muzzi was or what he did, or how I finally worked out Alberto R.'s role in the story. Things like that appear to leave him cold. (But then what doesn't? Cold's his stable state.) However, my talk with Father Daniel is an exception and he wants to know every single detail. Where were we? Were we in the gym? How were we dressed? What were we doing? Was it a formal confession between penitent and confessor or was it an informal chat? How far did I get before I suddenly clammed up? And what exactly was it that made me clam? When I said 'expression', did I mean Father Daniel's facial expression or a verbal expression that he used, and if so what was it?

Nosy as a judge. But that's what McShrink's brief with me boils down to really: answering these two fundamental questions that judges are also often faced with: one, how mad is this mad

101

little jerk? And two, how can I find a name for his mania with which I can feel comfortable?

In the end, I have no doubt, he will settle for Paranoia. That's the one I would choose myself in his position. My heart bleeds for my fellow psychos who are led away to Bedlam protesting their sanity of mind. The louder you shout, the madder you seem. I know it is insufficient, not to say tautological, to go on repeating that I knew because I knew, but what other proof have I to bring forward? If I hadn't retracted when I had, i.e. *before* either of us had said anything definite, I'd probably be dead by now. That's my only proof: that I am alive and telling my story.

How do you grasp things anyway from a fragment of discourse? Catch someone out? Rumble something fishy? It's never just the words, it's always the way they are spoken. I don't remember how far I'd got, whether I'd already said I'd discovered something terrible, or whether I was still sort of skirting round the admission, hampered by shyness, all I know is that suddenly I caught a flash of – yes, it was fear on Father Daniel's face: astonishment, terror even, and this ghastly, icy, spike went through me, and I knew with Cartesian certainty – *Timet ergo reus est* – that this man was in it too. Part of the plot.

Yes, wait, it's coming back now, it went like this. We were in the gym, our usual meeting place. I was sitting on the floor opposite him, and Father Daniel was on the rowing machine, rowing busily on air. I'd got to exactly this point, bursting point, and it had taken me a lot of getting there. I said – blurted – 'Father, I need your help, I must tell someone or I think I'll go bananas.' (With Americans I always slip into what I think is an American way of speaking, I can't help it, it's my psittacosis, my parrot disease.) 'I've discovered something to do with Adam, something so dreadful that I hardly know . . .'

And it was then that my trusted confessor and confidant betrayed himself. Just in the nick of time, before I blew it. His chin dropped, his hands dropped, the oar-bar dropped out of them and pinged back on the frame like a snapped elastic, his nice friendly pink face turned a shade of putty in a trice and he whispered to me aghast, '*What?* You've discovered *what?*'

Don't tell me that's a normal reaction, Doc. Don't tell me I was imagining things. Don't tell me it was me he was afraid of, either: of Benanas. No, he was afraid of what I was about to say.

Afraid? The man was panic-stricken. Or he'd have been craftier. I had taken him right off his guard.

I was off mine too, naturally, but it didn't show because I had been off it pretty well since the start of the conversation. And earlier too, for that matter, ever since the hook had hooked into me. The embarrassment, the hesitation, they were all in key. 'I . . . I have discovered . . . I have discovered . . .'

But what the blank had I discovered? I had to think of something, quick.

'I have discovered . . .' (oh well, here we go) '. . . that I had homosexual leanings towards Adam when he was alive, and that I've still got them.' Roll of bass drums, Poddapopom. But what else could I say of sufficient import? Wasn't so far from the truth either. Or was it? *(Still in two matters about it, eh, Bent-or-straight?)*

If he'd been reprieved from the electric chair one minute before switch-on, Father Daniel could hardly have shown more relief. His colour seeped gradually back, and after a few deep breaths and a fanning of his face he was able to take up his stroke again. It was me, now, whose colour was starting to drain. Neck-high in horror, and now naked before the enemy . . .

At this point in my story Dr Macpherson perks up and comments on it with an at-last-we're-getting-somewhere ring in his voice: 'Stroke, Neck, Naked. Those are very physical words you use there, Ben. Now, I'm not asking you to accept any of this, not yet, but just listen to what I'm going to suggest to you and let it, so to speak, find a temporary resting place in your mind. Don't banish it, don't fight against it, just let it settle there . . .'

Oh, cribbage, here we go with the interpretations. I could say them all for him and spare him the trouble. The 'evil priest' is me. Or part of me. The terrible secret that I have to carry around with me unaided is my repressed homosexuality. Rather than accept the fact that I'm gay I have concocted this incredible tale of murder and conspiracy and betrayal played out in a religious setting. In reality the dead child is another part of me that the evil priest part has suffocated . . .

Cribbage and garbage. I'll be dropping out of therapy soon if this is all I can get from it: a story as crazy as my own, but with a much smaller cast. Of course it's possible that the business of Father Daniel's involvement in the conspiracy is something I imagined. I sometimes think so myself. I never had proof, never. Not even when, during my later confessions, I sent up little trial balloons to see if he was functioning as a channel. But the conspiracy itself existed. Oh yes, in its corporate, incorporeal way, it existed as solidly as the pyramids of Egypt.

This nerve-racking episode with Father Daniel left me so fearful of making further blunders that for a few days I was unable to continue my detective work. I didn't even dare to consult the files. I felt like a snail: a weaponless, timid creature, housed in a fragile shell, with scarcely the will to peek outside it, let alone to deploy my antennae. Snails, however, are by nature tough, rubbery little beasts, and fortunately I must also have shared some of their consistency, because gradually my spring came back; enough of it, at any rate, to enable me to embark on a second round of criss-cross telephoning. You can telephone without quitting cover, if you're careful, and I was.

I will set down the facts that I discovered on the grid of Adam's original list. That way, it seems easier to test their solidity:

San Giacomo –	Only other hospital in centre with a maternity department. Scrapped in favour of the right one, namely the underlined:
<u>San Giovanni all'Isola</u> –	The site of the crime.

That's the names accounted for, now for the row of telephone contacts:

06/3626663 –

Tel. no. of San Giacomo. No use. Scrapped also. (And then recovered later from the telephone directory. I'm always doing that: throwing away things I may need.)

06/6880117 –

Tel. no. of the laboratory at the San Giovanni all'Isola hospital where the urine specimens of all in-patients were analysed, the Lulli baby included. I checked, but couldn't find out any more than that for fear of arousing suspicion. The man with the tired voice sounded perkier this time around and, before coughing up any more info, wanted to know my name and on whose account I was ringing. *Fa niente, fa niente*, I flustered, *Grazie e arrivederci*, and hung up quick.

Alessia –

Computer assistance. Their technician turned out to be a girl called Patrizia Franchi, who introduced herself straight away as Patty. She had shown Adam – or so I inferred by the lightning way in which she denied it, practically before I'd even asked her – if not how to hack outright into someone else's computer, then at least how to perform some rather dodgy manoeuvres. (*Escusatio non petita, accusatio manifesta*, as Inigo likes to say.)

105

Admittedly, I was going on a hunch, but the hunch was strong and still is. Got nothing else out of her apart from this, and, later, a helpful suggestion about e-mailing that came to nothing. She was a loner, unconnected to the other names on the list.

Paolo (pal of G.) –

The Dante expert. Didn't find out anything more of interest from him either. He hadn't discovered who G. was, and consequently nor did I, ever. Like Patty he had no links to any of the other names on the list. The only one he had heard of, and that very vaguely, was Muzzi, who he said was a luminary. (That was the way he talked.)

Alberto R. –

Alberto Rossi, wannabe journalist. It was difficult to figure out where he fitted in when he didn't even know himself, but when I mentioned the name Lulli to him and the name of the hospital, the penny finally dropped, and out of the Rossi juke-box came a very interesting tune. A few days before Christmas, he said, he had received a telephone call from a Catholic weekly, calling itself *Nostri Figli*. They had asked him to do some research for them on the first child to be born in the centre of the capital after midnight on December 25th. (Bingo, *bingone*, and right in the bull's pupil.) Allegedly they ran a similar piece every year, only this millennium year they wanted to do a slightly longer article. He had done the research – no trouble really, there were only two hospitals to cover. (I knew that already, Buster, they're written at the top of this list: San Giacomo and San Giovanni all'Isola.) Nursing homes were all in the residential areas, and the Santo Spirito, although it was central, didn't have a maternity ward. All he'd had to do was make a couple of phone calls and take a few notes, do a little snooping around the hospitals the next day, and that was it. Later the magazine had rung back, he had given them the information, they had assured him they would send him his fee by post – 700,000 lire, not bad for four bus trips and two local phone calls – and that was the last he had heard of them. No money, no magazine either. *Nostri Figli* didn't exist. He assumed it was someone playing a joke on him. A telephone prankster. Wasn't me, by any chance, was it?

Paola Serra –

Nothing else important from her either at this point except that she confirmed Rossi's story for me. A journalist had in fact telephoned the hospital the night of December 24th/ 25th, wanting to know about births, and several others had called on the night of the 31st. New Year's Eve was typical, it happened every year, Christmas was a bit more unusual. But then it was the millennium. (It was indeed.)

H.R. –

Humility Rosenfeld. From her I learnt the following, regarding her fellow doctor Muzzi:

Dr Carlo Muzzi –

The luminary was a urologist. A specialist, therefore, with both knowledge of, and access to, infected specimens of urine. He was also member of a traditionalist, right-wing, Catholic lay organisation, on the lines of the Opus Dei, called The Knights of Acre. And The Knights of Acre (I tracked them down on the Internet later), amongst other things, did volunteer hospital work, sometimes in collaboration with – guess who? – the Ordine Ospitaliero di Santa Marta: the very same nursing order to which Sister John of God belonged. (Belonged or had belonged? Where was she, the urine-swapper and/or smotherer and hook-placer? South Georgia? Saint Helena? Reposing, like a Mafia victim, in a pillar of cement?)

Sister John of God –

Another negative proof, but proof all the same. Who placed her in that job in the hospital on the island while the Lulli baby was there???????? And who spirited her away afterwards so efficiently that neither Adam nor I, nor anyone else, could ever trace her???????? The convent was so darn cagey when I phoned that the string of question marks remained. But so did the fact that it takes an organisation to do things like that, and a fairly widespread one too. (Consider as additional proof the episode of the happy snappers – we'll come to that one later.)

Lulli –

In the end I only managed to question young Signora Lulli on one more point before she sent me packing. Had she or her husband spoken to any other priest at the hospital besides Adam? Her answer was skimpy but intriguing. Spoken, no, she said, but one evening another priest had put his head round the door and asked if she wanted to speak to him, and she had sent him away. The regular hospital chaplain, she imagined, doing his rounds. Name, appearance – she had noticed nothing special, remembered nothing. All she could say was that this other priest was a good bit older than Adam and not nearly as nice-looking. As regards nationality, she couldn't swear to it, but she thought on reflection that he must have been Italian or she would have noticed the foreign accent. Though perhaps not, because he didn't say much, she didn't let him. Tall or small? On the small side, yes, definitely on the small side.

And that's the contacts dealt with too. Next the four queries at the bottom of the list:

Are there nursing homes in centre? Check. –

I had, and so had Alberto Rossi: there were none.

Urine/eyedrops/
heart condition –
which? –

The first, urine. In order to detain his victim in hospital the murderer had definitely used the stratagem of infected urine.

Dante: eclipse =
power vacuum?
Check. –

I had, and so had Adam: it did. A solar eclipse corresponded to a black-out of the powers of good, a lunar eclipse to a black-out of the powers of evil.

Date? Probably trad.
but check. –

No problem here. Trad. stood for traditional: Christ's traditional date of birth. And Adam's surmise was right: the conspirators were traditional people, they had plumped for December 25th as the birthdate of the Antichrist. Hence poor little dead Antichrist Lulli.

And that was it. All that was left was the last and most mysterious item on the list, which yielded nothing in the way of knowledge, but I'll give it anyway for completeness' sake:

Check out Shorty –

Check him out? How could I check him out when I didn't know who he was? Shorty was the one name which had tormented me from the start and with which I had got nowhere at all. Nobody else seemed able to enlighten me now that Adam was no longer around to do so; no one had a clue who he was – no one on the list and no one off it. There were no Shorties in college (Father Julian was predictably known as Sneezy, on account of the hayfever), no Shorties in the University, no Shorties, as far as I could make out, in the whole of Rome, and maybe Italy. Oh, Adam, why weren't you a bit more explicit in your notes?

And why aren't you a bit more imaginative in your top storey? Is it because you haven't got one, Bengalow? You're not quite through with the list yet, there's still the poem. Read it and DO WHAT IT SAYS:

```
I give you the end of a golden string,
Only wind it into a ball:
It will lead you in at Hades' gate
Built in Jerusalem's wall.
```

QED. Not taken singly, perhaps, but the sum of these proofs seems to me, even now, close on incontrovertible. McShrink, however, follows his own path: the one with the crazy paving. 'On your own admission, though, Ben, the proofs are all negative. Your confessor said nothing, except to ask you what you had discovered; the computer woman admitted nothing, merely spoke a bit too quickly for your taste. You never looked for this Sister

John woman very thoroughly, either, did you? A telephone call to the Convent, a few questions to the hospital staff, and then you gave up. And it's the same with the other investigations: they're all tentative, all lukewarm, as if throughout you were trying to defend your theory, not to expose it to the rigours of proof.'

Hark who's talking about rigours of proof. Never read his Karl Popper or, as a squidgy soft scientist, he wouldn't be so jaunty. Doesn't it strike me as significant that my probes were so cautious? What a question. Of course it's significant. It's significant of my terror and my wish to stay alive. Why didn't I investigate more thoroughly? I'd like to have seen him in my position. Why didn't I put an ad in the paper while I was about it, listing everything I'd discovered so far and asking witnesses to come forward? Why didn't I put up a notice outside the seminary gate: MURDER SITE. ANYONE WITH INFORMATION TO CONTRIBUTE PLEASE CONTACT BEN, ROOM 24, EVENINGS AFTER 8 P.M.? The child was dead, Adam was dead and, for all I knew, Sister John of God was dead too: I was in a multicoloured funk and I wanted to survive.

Besides, there's a flaw in old McShrink's logic. Perhaps I *am* paranoid, perhaps the stress under which I lived made me suspect everyone in the end. But even if I am and even if it did, it *still* doesn't mean the conspiracy didn't exist. Look at Rousseau: he had paranoia, and on top of it he was hounded like a prey by his enemies his whole life long. The one thing doesn't exclude the other. PARANOID REPRESSED HOMOSEXUAL UNCOVERS FANATIC RELIGIOUS MURDER GANG – there's nothing contradictory in that, it's just unlikely. But then so's the world, comets, mankind, black holes, seahorses, kangaroos, cricket regulations and everything you can name. If likelihood was the benchmark of truth we'd all be liars.

HE MADE THE STARS ALSO

It's funny, when we were finally allotted our pastoral work and the soup kitchen fell to me and Phil, I reckoned we'd drawn a short straw. So did everyone else. And yet, in this grey period of stasis between nightmares, it was the soup kitchen that saved me.

The soup kitchen and Stella. What a name: Stella, the Star. It had no worrying connotations for me then and why should it have done? 'The name of the star is called . . .' just that, as far as I knew. And its owner just the heavenly/earthly body that lit up my life when most it needed lighting. Are the fires of Hell that warm, that bright? If they are I'll go down like Don Giovanni: head first, no fear and no regrets.

Oh, Ben, you miserable git, what *are* you saying? This whole Stella business gets so out of proportion in my memory. I inflate it and colour it and knead things into it, both for good and for bad, until I almost convince myself that she and I had some kind of proper relationship going – sentimental, I mean, reciprocal, two-way flow. Whereas, if I'm to be brutally honest (which I must be if I'm ever to come out of this tangle), whatever traffic there was between us was pretty light really, and ran always in one and the same direction: from me to her, from me to her.

Significant of this is the fact that my diary picks up again on the exact day that I met her. Or let's say the day that I first saw her, because meetings, like relationships, are two-sided things – you don't meet a wall, you run into it, so, better still, then, on the day that I ran into Stella. That's when my diary starts again, and with the following brief entry. Which, nevertheless, is eloquent in its spare little way:

June 12th, 2001.

Twinkle, twinkle.

I had to keep things short because the diary came with me
everywhere now, tucked into the back pocket of my jeans: there
was nowhere I dared leave it. (Pity I couldn't have stored the discs
there, too, but I was afraid of squashing them.) The next entry,
however, written a few days later, is a little longer, and the mood
upbeat in a way that only a week earlier would have been
unthinkable:

June 17th, 2001.

*Must have inherited some of Mum's Gore-Tex skin-layers
after all. Small things in life still seem worth living for.
Can't pray, can't work, can't sleep much, can't <u>stomach</u>
Hegel - cheerless old megalomaniac - but who cares?
Bought two Bounty bars today. Scoffed one and took the
other one to the shelter and gave it to the little crusty girl,
Stella, and watched her as she ate it. 'Sei fantastico', she
told me, coconut was her favourite food, practically the
only thing she could always fancy. How come I was so
clever? How come I was so sweet? Well, okay, Italian is a
flowery language compliment-wise, and I noticed she
slipped half a bar to the dog when she thought I wasn't
looking, but still. Fantastico. Bravo. Dolce. No one's ever
called me any of those things before, in any lingo. Don't
know why, when they were different sexes and nationalities
and sizes and he was so clean and vital and she is so lazy
and grubby, but she reminds me of Adam: maybe it's the
way she perches on things, all hunched and spiky, with her*

neck jutting out one way and shoulder blades the other.
Or maybe it's the don't-care swagger. She's not much of a
conversationalist, and has the manners of an autistic
marmoset, but I'm happy just to watch her. Must find out
more about anorexia from Father Quentin, and about
bulimia and how they mesh. And maybe mug up a bit on
the Rome drug scene.

A couple of weeks later there's even a stab at a poem – heavy
Tolkien influence discernible, elves regrettably much to the fore.
But there's no way I'm going to include that for McShrink's
inspection. So, back to the soup kitchen and the summer and
autumn months of 2001. A lull, an intermezzo before the mad
winter waltz struck up again. I spent two evenings a week there,
in theory learning how to act as shepherd to this bedraggled
flock, but in fact just one more black sheep milling around with
the others, only slightly bossier and much, much busier. Phil I
trusted, more than I trusted anyone else in the community, which
was not much but it was something; Don Rocco, the Italian priest
who ran the place, I trusted too. (Within slightly narrower limits:
I was a bit wary of Italian-speaking priests after what Signora
Lulli had said about the visitor. OK, she was probably right and
he was just a hospital chaplain doing his rounds, but the bilingual
Don Anselmo had me worried sick all the same.) The rest of the
company were tramps, drop-outs, drug addicts, and beached
immigrants who hadn't made it, plus the usual handful of semi-
professional loafers up for any kind of freebies, and all of them I
trusted *without* limit. Whatever else they might have done they
hadn't killed Adam or a two-week-old baby, and they weren't
going to kill me either, or not immediately. Thus my two evenings
a week were a picnic in comparison to the remainder of my time.
A picnic, and after the arrival of Stella, a picnic by starlight.

In college I lived like a soul in limbo. Low profile, lower spirits.
My investigations had reached a point of no return and also a

point of no advance. I knew now, as fully as I would ever know without catching the culprits and obtaining a confession, what had happened: there was this group of religious maniacs, chiliast cranks, neo-Albingensian eschatologists or whatever you like to call them, who had concocted a crackpot theory of the coming of the Antichrist and had acted – drastically, pitilessly – in order to prevent its fulfilment. They had identified the baby on their crazy criteria, kept it on in hospital by a ruse so that they could get at it conveniently, slaughtered it at the time they considered propitious, forced a ritual hook into its little dead cheek (if not into its live one. I wouldn't have put it past them, though I suppose it would have been a bit too noisy and risky), and then pushed Adam off the roof when he discovered their crime and threatened to disclose them. Literal interpretation of the Apocalypse went out with Saint Augustine: the Catholic Church harbours a lot of harker-backers, it's hospitable that way, but this group beat them all.

I lived also like a victim of slow poisoning. They say people become dull and listless as the poison eats into them, and the poison that was eating into me was fear and mistrust – of virtually all the people I lived with or had contact with in the course of the day. Adam had tussled with them – him, her, whoever it was. I thought back on the night noises, the din, the arguments: for some reason, perhaps because he'd had to, or perhaps because he hadn't feared them sufficiently or understood them right, he had confronted them openly. I was not going to make the same mistake. I had very nearly made a slip there in the gym with Father Daniel; I was not going to do so again. Shadow and immobility were my safeguards. I must make no moves at all, send out no signs, carry on exactly as I always had done. Study, Greg, gym, confession, weekly letter to Mum, All's well, all's well; study, Greg, gym, confession, weekly letter to Mum, All's well, all's well. All's hell. Ping-pong defeat on Saturday at the hands of Inigo. Sunday blow-out (which stuck in my throat: I was getting thinner fast), spot of chess or telly and back to Monday again. Boring little Ben, but cautious, unnoticed and, above all, still-alive-and-kicking little Ben. Funny, we thought we might make something out of him, now it'll be a parish at the most.

The only way I could break the deadlock, and this was horribly clear to me, was by laying a trap and baiting it with some irresistible bait. To catch a tiger you tie a goat to a tree and wait for him to show his stripey nose. I had a tiger to catch but I very much didn't want to be the goat.

A few ideas had occurred to me, none of them very bright. Mentioning the Antichrist in a loud voice at dinner, for example, and watching for people's reactions. Daft: impossible to cull the reactions of so many in such a short time. Sounding out *in camera* Don Anselmo and my other chief suspects on the same topic. Dangerous, possibly lethal. Sending an anonymous e-mail to all addresses in our domain saying, You slew my cat's-paw, but watch out, I'll get even, signed, Satan. Unfeasible: no clue as to how it was done without leaving a trace. I'd seen a girl in a film do it in a computer shop but I knew it wouldn't work for me. Letting slip something – something but I wasn't sure what – to Father Daniel: rattling him again, this time a bit harder, and seeing if anything came out. I'd been waiting to see if the news of my homosexual leanings was going to filter through to anyone in particular (with what repercussions I hardly dared imagine), but so far nobody had changed their attitude towards me – shown either concern or interest or anything else. Big relief.

And yet not. Because how long could I hold out in this untenable position? Knowing and not knowing, suspecting every-one and no one, terrified of moving and terrified of staying still. A fly in a web, if not devoured by the spider, is finally killed by desiccation, no? And this was what was happening to me: I was drying up, drying up inside for want of nourishment, want of faith – in God and in my fellow men.

And this was where the soup kitchen came in. A tiny toehold in a slithering, tumbling, crumbling universe. Everything I had held good might be rotting around me – OK, OK. My God might be dead, Adam too, my religion might be nonsense, my fellow priests might be murderers – OK, OK. There might be no afterlife, no reward, no revelation, no permanent values either, but at least when I handed out a plate of spaghetti to some hapless old hobo, or sat down with a group of the lads for a game of *scopa*, or listened to the ravings of some wonky old bird with Alzheimer's and got her to calm down a bit, I could tell myself that these things, now, today, were good things to do: that a happy, greedy old face was better than a sad, hungry one. That a peaceful mind was better than a seething one. That four men playing cards was not such a bad thing either, and that a world with these tiny puddles of light in it was still a world that contained something precious.

The enemy, of course, tried to take this away from me as well, dropped his poison over the soup kitchen the way he dropped it over my friendship with Adam, in the hope – (*Careful there with your metaphors, Ben Jonson, or you'll be leaving a drop but in the soup.*) OK, fusspot. But I won't let him poison anything. Far from 'flaunting her friendship at me', or whatever disgusting way he put it, Stella made no effort to win my notice at all. She made no effort to win anything, for that matter, and that was what touched my heart about her. I saw her as a loser, one of life's losers on a small unheroic scale that somehow makes the losses even sadder. Nothing to get worked up about: she'd just let things slip through her tattooed fingers till she was left empty-handed, save for a stringy lead that attached her to a black mongrel puppy with a spotted bandana round its neck. No job, no money, no friends except stammering P-P-Peppe, no future and not much recent past that she cared to remember either: just a haze of dope and the various turbid things she'd had to do to get it. (Best for her they remained turbid, I reckoned.) And all this at barely nineteen.

No, she made no efforts. We even had to feed the puppy. De-flea it, worm it, take it to have its shots. I volunteered for that: it was one of the few things I could do that seemed to bring her closer. For shelter we put the pair of them in with the Little Sisters of the Holy Raiment. Very fitting: Stella didn't have one item of clothing that wasn't punched through like a colander, and the dog was pretty mangy too. Once she had a bed we didn't even see her around that often any more; she just curled up on the mattress with the puppy and a set of headphones and the supply of Bounty bars I brought her and lay there. Getting her strength back, I suppose, her cells wriggling back to life after the bashing. Multiplying.

I think a lot about love these days. Romantic love, I mean, not fondness like I feel for Mum and the family, which is all mixed up with guilt anyway. One of my worst scenarios is Mum getting bedridden in her old age and me having to care for her, do intimate things for her like bring a bedpan or change her nightie; the sense of duty pulling one way and the sense of shame and nausea pulling the other would rend me asunder. But if what I felt for Adam is anything to go by – and for Stella too in a lesser way – the kind of love you fall into is not complicated like that. It doesn't snag you crossways, it pulls you, bodily, mentally, and totally happily, in one and the same direction: towards the beloved. Sex . . . ? I don't know much about it as a communication strategy, it's possible it upsets matters, but I have a sense that when things are right it doesn't. That nothing does. That, on the contrary, every shared activity, even things like going to the dentist or paying a parking fine at the post office, just serve to unite you, to tie you closer and closer.

I have felt the possibility of feeling this feeling, and some of the reality of feeling it too, once and a bit in my life to date. Will I ever feel it again? Long enough to know whether the other person feels it too? Who knows, but even as it is I count myself lucky. I wouldn't have it different. If God should exist, and if He should be Ben-benevolent and say to me, Look, Ben, here in My right palm are all the top females of My creation and all the top blokes, you can have a passionate, reciprocated love affair with whichever of them you choose, as many as you choose, for as long as you choose; and here in My left palm are these two odd skinny little creatures, Adam and Stella, whom you can love for a while from a distance without ever knowing if they love you back – no question, I'd settle for Adam and Stella. ('The damned *choose* evil, Benedict, of their own free will.' If these are its standard bearers you're darn right they do.)

I'm not sure Stella ever noticed me at all really, not until . . . well, not until she had to, and even then I don't think I was much of a person for her, more of an instrument. But anyway it didn't matter. It was enough to be around her, breathing the same air, sharing the same slice of time/space: walking into the soup kitchen with a flutter in my throat and wondering if I would spot her; skinning my ears for the sound of her drawly gruff voice with its brief barks which was practically all I ever heard it utter. *Suh, Nah, Mah, Che ne soh.* She was there. I could relax and let my insides smile. McShrink says I used her to replace my missing love object, but when I said, 'What love object? Adam?' he said, 'No, God': I needed a remote and ethereal being to replace my absentee God.

Honestly. A stoned, promiscuous, nineteen-year-old down-and-out in place of a deity. For me the love of God is guilt-ridden, too, worse than Mum's. And how can you feel protective of a God? Want to fatten a God? Shield a God from adversity? No, Shrinko, that's not the way to read it. If you want to get structuralist, Stella was more like my child. Or more like a brother, say; the brother that I'd failed to save. She was thin as a stick insect, like Adam was, only in her case the thinness was even more accentuated, more touching. Her skin was sallow and furry like the husk of a fresh almond, less green, but only by a shade. Her head, when she first fished up, was shaven, but as the hair began to grow back in again it started sprouting the same soft golden ring as Adam's. (Their halos, oh, yeah, their anti-halos.) I don't know what psychological undercurrents she stirred in me, and don't much want to: guilt, power craving, repressed lust, McShrink can take his choice; the fact remains that I would have torn my breast pelican-style to

122

nourish her, I truly think I would. I'd have given a limb to pull her out of the bog into which she'd sunk. My soul? Well, willingly I'm not so sure, but perhaps I'd have given that too in the end. And perhaps that's just what I did.

Anyway I spent the summer under the aegis of this dusty little star: thinking about her, caring for her, watching out for her and over her, and letting very little else come into my mind. The else was too troubling.

In July, however, this deliberately laid-back policy failed me for a few weeks and I worked myself up willy-nilly into a great and useless stew. Boiling outside and boiling in. With the closure of the Greg for summer vac the community went into its annual retreat and we had readings at mealtimes instead of talk. Reading was an unpopular task – you ate after everyone else had finished, and after most of the food was finished too – so predictably it fell to us tads. The only bright aspect was that we could choose what text we liked, within reason. The opportunity, tiger-wise, seemed too good to miss: I could play peek-a-boo with the brute, if I dared, stick my neck out just a few millimetres and then sit back and watch as he stuck his out in return – hopefully that much further.

I not only could do this but must. I was betraying Adam now on two fronts, the front of affection and the front of revenge, and it was time I stopped. I was weak and cowardly and inconstant. Bad Ben.

I worked hard on my plan. I spent hours in the library, tracking down useful bits and pieces of material and then photocopying them and bringing them back to my room, where I worked further, kneading them into a whole. Into tiger bait. I was going to make it, yes, irresistible. I decided to begin with two recent opinions on the legend of the Antichrist, the first from Wilhelm Bousset, 1925, who declared that it was

. . . now to be found only among the lower classes of the Christian community, among sects, eccentric individualists and fanatics.

The second from Norman Cohn, 1957, who saw it likewise as belonging to

the obscure underworld of popular religion.

Smack in the old baby-face for Father Simon, should the tiger happen to be him. But I wasn't going to leave it there, no, no, no, nor even continue on that track. This was where the cunning came in. After that I was going to do an abrupt U-turn and start reading the final chapter of Bernard McGinn's masterly modern study of the Antichrist, where he examines the relevance of the legend to contemporary Christianity: Bultmann and the 'Antichrist within', Jung and 'the dark side of the psyche', Ricoeur and the recycling of ancient symbology into the credo-package of today. Very avant-garde stuff, intellectually speaking; Adam would have been proud of me. Last and best of all, *if* I could do it convincingly, I was going to tack on a piece of my own composing, linking the Antichrist, the arch-deceiver, with things like food ads on telly, where salami comes in packets from the sky, and eggs from happy virtual chickens scrabbling around on the digital grass of 'Rainbow Farm'. The predominance of appearance over substance in today's electronic culture – all things bright and beautiful, the special effects guys made them all. Touch on pollution too, global warming, water shortage, consumerism, loss of traditional values, etc., as predicted in the Apocalypse. Armageddon and Battle of Seattle. If that didn't catch the interest of an Antichrist buff, what would?

I had it all planned and ready, my tiger trap. The lectern in the refectory is raised: you look down on the eaters, while they have to tilt their heads right back to look at you. I would be able to see them all and observe every little movement. And someone would make a movement once I touched on my theme, I knew they would, and it wouldn't be such a little movement either, it would be quite a big one. A start, maybe even a jump – they wouldn't be able to hide it. They would look up, and our eyes would meet, and at last I would find myself face to face with this loathsome creature I had been chasing after in my mind for so long. It would be like smoking out vermin from a bolt hole. One swoop and, Gotcha!

Thus the theory. In the end and in the practice, typical me, I read from the *Confessions* of Saint Augustine instead – the first book I hit upon as I made my way to the refectory, empty-handed and in a panic, having dumped my carefully prepared script in a dustbin en route. I funked it again, missed my chance. Sorry Adam, but I'm not ready to join you in your vertical churchyard, not just yet. He'll look up at me all right, your murderer, and I'll recognise him for what he is, but he'll recognise me too for what I am: namely, next on the death list.

Adam got his own back, however, because the *Confessions* fell open at book four, chapter four, and I found myself reading aloud about the death of Augustine's beloved friend in phrases such as the following:

> Yet in a moment, before we had reached the end of the first year of a friendship that was sweeter to me than all the joys of life as I lived it then, you took him from this world. For you are the God of vengeance . . .
>
> All that we had done together was now a grim ordeal without him. My eyes searched everywhere for him, but he was not there . . .

Served me right. I even had to read the bit where Augustine admits that, no matter how much he loved him, he hasn't got the courage to give up his life for his friend. And that was my position: I just didn't have the guts. My anger was drying up, like everything else, and without anger I was gutless. I didn't even have the guts to opt out, either. I knew what would happen: I would jog along like this for . . . however long it took for exasperation to set in in place of paralysis, and then I would leave. Defeated, crestfallen, the way a disease leaves an organism.

I would never avenge Adam, never solve the riddle, never be a priest and never be a proper layman either. I would leave the college and go rudderless home to Mum, and I would never hear the end of it.

AND HE SENT FORTH A RAVEN

At the beginning of autumn, without so much as a thank you or goodbye, Stella drifted off again, and I touched a new low. Bump. OK, our relationship was all in my head, all one-sided, but nevertheless it felt like a betrayal. The faithful P-P-Peppe continued to drop in regularly for meals, however, and through him I got news of her, enough to keep me consoled and going. She was off the drugs – for good now – she was eating, she was putting on a little weight, the puppy ditto. The doc is right: I require very little of my love objects, chiefly that they should simply stay alive, and possibly healthy into the bargain. The rest is just icing.

But I am not healthy, Ben Judas. I am rotting dead, in case you've forgotten. All this love business is hogwash: you've never loved anyone, you're still in the crush stage. First a crush on me, and now a crush on this nauseating little junkie who barely realises you exist . . . Remember me, for Antichrist's sake. Remember your promise. REMEMBER TO CHECK OUT SHORTY.

And remember Saint Augustine and his cowardice. And remember the Gospel: Smaller love than this no man hath that he won't even keep a promise to his dead friend. In shame I turned to the computer and set about carrying out my second plan, viz. the sending of an e-mail message, the text of which I had honed in the meantime to a form which I reckoned was as safe as anything I could possibly devise. But would I ever actually dare to mail it?

As a step in the right direction I got in touch with Patty again. How could someone send a message to all the addresses in a given domain without knowing each single recipient's individual address? Was there a way of carpet-sending, so to speak, along the lines of carpet-bombing? And if there was, how could this someone send their message without their own address showing up on the screen?

Well, she said – very professional, not a trace of curiosity or surprise, but I suppose she was getting used by now to our spying seminarist ways – carpet-sending, no, but in every domain there was always one computer with a default set-up: this person, whoever he was, could send his message without specifying the recipient's name, and it would automatically land up in the default postbag. It would then be up to the user of the default computer to pass the message on to all the others. That's what fans of famous people usually did: sent e-mails to Madonna@ virgin.net, for example, in the hope that the secretary or whoever was at the other end would pass the message on.

The example puzzled me for a sec. It was the combination that did it; I know perfectly well Madonna is a pop star. What a mug. Luckily Patty didn't seem to notice. The other question, she went on, was easier. How to send anonymously: well, there were various ways but the safest thing to do was to register with one of those big net services like Hotmail, giving a fake name and address, and then send the message from there. In theory computers always leave a trace, but in practice it would be very hard, almost impossible, for anyone to pick it up and work their way back to the computer from which the message came.

So. Safe in practice. Was safe in practice enough? It had to be. And, then, well, so what. Even if the enemy with his henchmen at every corner *did* manage to trace the computer it would only put him in the same position I was in: one computer with forty-two-plus possible users. Why pick on me in particular? Why boring Ben? (Well, the discs had been found in my cupboard, for one thing, and Adam was my friend, for another. Still, that didn't really signify . . . Or did it and would it?)

Best quit dithering or I'd never get anywhere. I registered with Hotmail under the name of Idol Shepherd, code name Spoiler. My hands shook while I did so and my fingers kept hitting the wrong keys and it took me ages. The message, when I finally tapped it out, ran as follows:

    Talk about no dithering; I hesitated a quasi-eternity before clicking on the mailing icon. Could any harm come of this plan? No. At worst, no good might come of it, but no harm either. Could I be *sure* on this head? Yes, I could. I had chosen the meeting place carefully: market place, Saturday, people, confusion; a bar on the corner of the piazza with a good view of the statue, and a billiard room in the back, with a lav I could bolt into like the coward I was, should my quarry suddenly turn hunter and come after me instead. Ferret/tiger after rabbit/snail/goat. (I'll have to watch it with the animal metaphors, or Adam will be back again to carp. Carp – isn't that typical?) The message itself seemed to me impossible to improve on. Meaningless for anyone other than the intended recipient, and yet not so meaningless that a person receiving it by chance would feel authorised to trash it on the spot. The 'macroscopically' lent it gravitas, I felt. For the *true* recipient, on the other hand, should it manage to reach him, it should be not only chock-full of meaning but hopefully fear-engendering meaning and menace as well. He should feel breath on his neck and the stab of failure in his heart, if he had one. He should feel obliged – no, stronger, forced – to react in some way to the threat, at least to the extent of turning up in an oblique fashion at the meeting place. I didn't expect him under the statue, mind you, but I expected – provided I turned up early enough, and left late enough, and watched closely enough – to catch a glimpse of him lurking around somewhere in the vicinity. The non-existent magazine; the 'wrong subject'; the implication that perhaps the sender of the message knew the 'right' one. He would *have* to follow up on that, surely? He – she, they, whichever – couldn't afford not to.

*   *   *

First shame at doing too little, then panic at having done too much: the message went up on the notice board, slap in the middle like a banner. Printed out and pinned there in full view of all, with a red circle round it and an arrow and a question mark. No, two question marks. 'QUIS??' I sent it on the evening of September 5th – had to leave a bit of time for it to get through to the enemy, but not enough to allow him to prepare a counter-move – and on the morning of the 6th, there it hung.

Done it. No going back. (Although still open to me was the option of not going forward either: I didn't *have* to go to the piazza, did I? Yes, I funking well did.) The next two nights I hardly managed to sleep at all, I was so wound up. And when I did sleep it was to dream dreams that wound me even tighter. I didn't remember the content of them except, vaguely, one of a chase that took place in a Shanghai tube station, but the anguish on waking was such that the return to reality was almost a relief. The real murderer, after all, could only kill me once, and judging from his track record he was likely to do it quickly. The dream demons operated under no such constraints.

I drank a fruit juice at breakfast on the morning of the 8th, and then a cup of black coffee, and sicked them both up in the bathroom afterwards. (All mine now, the bathroom, but not for much longer: with the imminent arrival of the new tadpoles Adam's room was being prepared for a new occupant. I resented the presence there even of the cleaner.)

There was a big summer seminar in progress next door *chez* the

132

Americans, which we were all supposed to attend, in preparation for next year – a seminal summer seminar on semantics for seminarists in the seminary – no, I'm being silly, it was on the Pauline Corpus: exegesis thereof. But I simply couldn't face it. I truanted and took a bus and blundered through the streets of old Rome instead. Found myself at some point in front of the Caravaggios in Piazza del Popolo: *there's* a Pauline Corpus for you, and a smashing Equine Corpus too. But I was barely able to look at them, I had to keep consulting my watch and counting the minutes till blast off.

At half-past ten I started walking, and by eleven I was already installed in the café with a newspaper and a cuppa cheeno and a pair of dark specs and a woolly beret like an eggcosy, which was all I had been able to find in college in the hat line. Underneath it my brains coddled, truly like an egg.

I thought I'd thought of everything, but of course the two most important things I hadn't thought of at all. One, there was only one exit in the café where there should have been two; and two, cafés in Italy are places of transit and quick turnover, and long-sitting guests are not appreciated unless they reorder. And reorder. And reorder.

The lav was to hand, OK, but I couldn't use it for fear of missing my tiger. My poor bladder, I reckon I stretched it permanently out of shape that day. I didn't have much money on me either, or I'd have downed more solids as blotting. Cuppa cheeno, glassa mineral water, then, as midday drew near, a beer to steady the nerves, and a second one a quarter of an hour later because I found it worked.

Great mistake. By half-past twelve my legs were twisted round each other like a Rodin statue, and still no sign of a familiar figure, or an in any way suspicious one. Poor Bruno on his pedestal was piled around with empty fruit crates, as if for another roasting. No one hung out in his vicinity: steer clear of heretics always. The market was in full swing, customers came and went, but none seemed to linger on after their business was done and none seemed to be unduly curious. There were a few tourists ambling about, mostly Japanese, taking the odd snapshot and eating ices. I saw a nun with a shopping basket at one point and nearly toppled from my seat, but all she did was shift around the stalls, picking up onions and whatnots and packing them into her basket, her head demurely bent. If it had been her she'd have been bound to glance around her, suss out the scene like I was doing, but, no, her attention was all on her task. The stallholders looked as if they knew her, too, smiled at her as to a regular customer.

So, no, not the nun. But if not the nun, then who? Taxis drove through the piazza, Vespas too. Perhaps the tiger was motorised? I hadn't thought of that either, Dumbo. Nor of the possibility that he might be lurking in the wings as I was myself: sitting immobile at the window of an upper storey, for example, scanning the scene through a pair of binoculars, waiting, waiting.

Well, he'd have to blinking wait. And that made two of us. At a quarter to two I could hold out no longer on the liquid front. I made a dash for the lav: it was occupied. I dashed back to do another quick pan of the piazza and earned myself another strange look from the barman, who'd given me several already. What *was* this little camouflaged weirdo up to? I smiled at him foolishly and foolishly ordered yet another drink: an espresso this time. He sighed like one who has seen it all, twice over. '*Un espresso? OK, Batman.*'

Out of the corner of my eye I noticed the occupant was leaving the lav now, so I raced there in relief and brushed past him into sanctuary. Another minute and I seriously think I might have been in for strangury. I was as quick as I could manage, but all the while I imagined I was missing the one vital moment of the whole vigil. When I got back to my table and my unwanted coffee, though, the scene still offered nothing especially promising, threatening or whichever. The stalls were closing down now, the vendors were sweeping up and heaping more kindling on poor Bruno's pyre, interrupted in their work by a few last-minute shoppers. The same little gaggles of camera-slung tourists hung around here and there, listless in the heat, but fewer of these, too, now that it was lunchtime.

I was draining my espresso grounds when a worrying thought came to me re the man in the lav, the one I'd almost bumped into in my haste. I hadn't paid any attention to him. Who was he? What had he been wearing? I hadn't noticed him enter the café earlier, and yet I'd been keeping check on all comers well before they crossed the threshold, just in case. How come this one had escaped me? Was he staff, or what? Had he looked at me in any particular way? I think he had. Yes, he had, he'd stared and raised his hands. Oh Michaelmas-daisies – it was coming up Michaelmas, incidentally – what if he'd been holding a hidden camera and had taken a photograph? That's exactly what I would have done had I been in the tiger's position: I would have kept well out of the way myself but I would have hired someone with a camera to go all round the square and into all the shops and bars and places and take photographs of everyone he saw there . . .

Yes, I'm a slow thinker all right. But when at last the insight came it came like a bolt. Photographs. Photographers. Of course, how could I have been so thick? The tourists – it was one of them, he had engaged one of them. And maybe not only one, maybe several. Everything else forgotten, I now began concentrating on the behaviour of the tourist groups – only two left now – and sure enough I hit centre. The nearer group was clearly bona fide: a family with Bushranger hats on, who seemed to be squabbling about what to see or where to eat. The father had a map out, and he and Mum were snatching it from one another and poring over it by turns, while the kids sat slumped on a flight of steps, squabbling over something else – a Walkman, I think. But the second group – oh, the second group. The second group was a couple of Asiatics, male and female, small and totally unremarkable to my hasty Western eyes, whom I would normally have classified as Japanese (and probably already had, probably they were the same couple all along), but whom I now, on closer inspection, decided were more likely Indonesians. What was so odd about them? What clinched it for me that it was them? Well, the number of photographs they were taking, for one thing, and the way they took them. They stood towards the far end of the piazza but fairly central, which was odd in itself since there was no shade there, and to a careless observer, such as I had been before I cottoned on, they appeared to be taking souvenir photographs of each other against the various backdrops that the piazza offered, wheeling slowly round the 360 degrees like the hands of a clock. In actual fact, however, once you looked closely, you could see that what they were really doing was photographing the passers-by.

And the sitters-in too. They were keeping tabs on everyone – all the customers of the various bars and restaurants were faithfully snapped, one by one and totally unawares, as they went in and as they went out. The man would make a little pointing sign with his head, the woman would move to wherever he indicated, pretending to pose, and then, when the subject was in their lens, click.

The night when I'd been listening through the bathroom door to the computer noises and I'd heard the person on the other side stop and pause as if he too were listening out for me – at that moment I had felt this horrible living thread connecting us, like an umbilical cord, and it had terrified me. Now I felt it again. Not so taut, but I felt it, and again I felt – not quite terror, but strongish fear, a good deal stronger than the one I had come to live with on a daily basis. There – admittedly in the person of his deputies, but there all the same – stood the enemy. It's one thing to be after someone, it is another to find them, and it is another still to be found in your turn as you are finding. Were they snapping the customers of this café too?

You could bet they were. For all I knew they might even have a telescopic lens. But they weren't going to snap me, not if I stayed here till nightfall.

Heigho, I'd better resign myself. Another cuppa cheeno, *prego*.

* * *

136

As it turned out I was lucky: the happy snappers left shortly afterwards, and I paid up and went half an hour later, hugging the walls like an old B-movie sleuth with my eggcosy practically down to my chin. When I got back to college the first thing I did was to go into the kitchens to check how many people besides myself had lunched out, because, OK, lots of people usually did, that was one of my reasons for choosing a Saturday in the first place, but you never knew. What if this Saturday had been different? What if all the places had been full except for one – mine? It would have looked very fishy, not to say accusatory. Might as well have signed the flipping e-mail.

Sister Consuelo was in charge of catering that weekend. I found her mousing, of all things: crawling along the corridor that leads to the larders, poking under the shelves with a broom to draw the traps out. I knelt down alongside and helped her for a little while because it looked fun: a sabre-toothed mouse anyone can deal with.

When I asked about lunch she paused in her chase and gave me a funny piqued little look over the top of her hunting glasses. 'Whass he doing?' she said. 'Checkin' on me, or what? I tole him already: nineteen out, twenny-four in.'

Told who? Oho, I had been preceded.

'Tole him – Father Blaise. He was in here earlier, wantin' to know who was in, who was out, who here, who there. I tole him, Father, I can tell you how many meals we serve, how many plates we wash, I can't tell you who was itting off them. Organisesshun,' she sighed. 'We don't need no more, we got enough of that already.'

It was Pascal's duty to run a tight budget, and in fact only a couple of weeks later he introduced a war-on-waste system, long overdue, by which you had to sign a log-book if you were out for any particular meal. Coincidence? I couldn't tell, I only knew I could hardly bear to look at the man any more, let alone speak to him. My relations with Don Anselmo improved considerably as a result: like one of those weather clocks, out came figure A into the sunshine, and in went figure B with his umbrella into the dark.

Pascal and Michael, Blaise and Michael. Master and work-dog. In some accounts it is Michael – the Prince of the Citizens of Heaven – who is the slayer of the Antichrist. This Michael wasn't a Prince of anything, he was just a bustling, fawning lackey, ready to tell on anyone, report ill of anyone. An everyday stinker. But then evil *is* banal – look at the Nazis.

Nazis – that's not a comparison I thought up myself. Who said it, I wonder?

Hannah Arendt said it, Benal. But we're here to catch a murderer, not to play ruddy bourgeois parlour games.

YOUR EYES SHALL BE OPENED

The shape of this whole story, if I were to draw a graph of it, is like a flight of steps. Descending, naturally. But descending where? Why, into the good old Bottomless Pit, where else? Make the steps circular and you have a near approximation to Dante's rings of Hell.

The first big downward lurch came with Adam's death. (Tactless way of putting it? I know, pal, I'm sorry, but the metaphor requires it.) Then came the discs and the ferret, a shallow step, that, in comparison to the others. Then, woomph, down again brusquely: the finding of the Lulli baby, which put me on a level of anguish hitherto unimagined. I thought of that level as Limbo, I stayed there for a nasty while, with another little downwards slide when my Star deserted me. The heinous terrorist attack on America was unrelated to my small-scale drama – I cling to this firmly, despite the brayings of the millennium freaks, who immediately claimed it as one of their forecast catastrophes attendant on the birth of the Antichrist, trust them – but as we all sat glued to the World Service that day, absorbing more and more horrors, it was as if it, too, were dragging me lower. I was ashamed to be a member of this species of fatally flawed, confused and violent primates, bent on slaughtering one another in the name of a name. Christ is with us, Allah is with us, Yahweh is with us: would that He were not, I thought to myself, would that He never had been. And then I was ashamed of this thought, because faith is not the issue, it is when you lose *hope* in God that you really cross the divide; and then I was ashamed of my shame, in my usual tail-biting way, and ashamed – oh, simply of being alive and doing so little, and caring so much about the life of one as yet unborn child when people were dying at that moment in their thousands . . .

Let us pray, said the Rector, so I prayed: God, if You made us like this, unmake us and remake us. And Chance, if you made us like this, make it so that one day we stop praying and learn to unmake and remake ourselves. A terrible prayer for *me* to utter, but perhaps not such a terrible prayer.

In October the academic year at the Greg picked up again and I stumbled on, attended my lectures, churned out my essays – my own stuff, I couldn't use Adam's any more, didn't dare. I felt a bit easier with Don Anselmo now I'd focused my suspicions on Pascal and Michael, and he was a bit easier with me – more tolerant, less critical. Inigo had fallen Outigo with him of late, don't quite know why. Phil said the business of Archbishop Milingo had lowered his stock, but I think this was meant as a joke.

Mid-November Peppe came shambling in with the news that Stella was living with a group of fellow crusties in a squat somewhere near San Lorenzo. She was putting on quite a lot of weight now, he said with his sweet, contorted, stammerer's smile, because she was *in-in-incinta*, ex-ex-expecting. The baby was due in February sometime. He brought with him a little note she had written for Don Rocco and the nuns: 'Forgive me, *miei cocchetti*, for leaving you like that. I was so ashamed. I wanted to get rid of the baby and was afraid you wouldn't let me. Now I'm going to keep it. I'll bring it in to show you one day. Think you'll like it better than the puppy. Love to everyone and thanks for all the help, Stella.'

Cocchetti was such a funny, tender word in the context. Slightly patronising, too; protective: a term you might use to a bunch of kids or mentally handicapped adults. Perhaps that's what we were to her, with our naïve outlook on the world: a bit of both.

The message tranquillised me, however, and on two counts: first, I no longer felt the sting of betrayal so strongly, because, after all, Stella hadn't just debunked and forgotten us; there had been a valid motive for her leaving, and a valid motive also for her not saying why. And second, maternity foils the death wish for a while, or so statistics say; holds it at bay at least up to the birth, and often beyond, so I reckoned that even without me to mount guard over her, Stella was in safe-keeping for the time being. The embryo would hold her firm, like an in-board sheet anchor.

Moment of relative calm all round, therefore, so that when the next step came, as it did soon afterwards, I was not in the least expecting it. Although I suppose you could say I was looking for it – in a desultory way. I had graduated to my own computer now, and every so often, in the intervals between study, I would fiddle around with the mad mass of material that I had accumulated. My forays into field-work had all met with failure – who knows, perhaps more desk work would yield something. Sooner or later.

I tracked down the Fatima Falange site on the Internet and all the millennium sites and what have you that were mentioned in Adam's files, and generally hopped around a bit, using things like Antichrist and Prophecy and Parousia as my keywords, sometimes singly, sometimes coupling them. It didn't seem to lead me anywhere, and it was a chore, because I had to cover my tracks like a hunted animal, and several of the sites I didn't dare enter using my own computer but had to change to the communal one. (Patty's warning had stuck about every computer always leaving its trace.) In the end I felt guilty about the expense and stopped. But now and again, say Saturday evenings, when the thought of the common room and the ping-pong and the watery coffee sometimes flattened me, I would have another quick bash.

One evening at the start of December – oh, fry my eyes, why didn't I do it earlier or not at all? – I entered the word Shorty.

I couldn't check Shorty out, maybe, but I certainly thought about him often enough. He haunted me, the little beggar.

Whirr, whirr. Shorty's skateboards. Shorty's hardware. Ras Shorty, pioneer of Soca music. What was Soca music? Talk about being in a backwater. Maybe something to do with football? Then a vaguely racy-looking site: Welcome, stranger, click on

'Browse'. I did. Welcome again, click 'Man' or 'Woman'. I did, I clicked 'Man'. Click again: 'Man looking for women' or 'Man looking for men'. Oh dear, my chronic dilemma, I lost courage and bolted.

But after a pause, I started up again and entered Shorty + Antichrist. Nothing: the combo seemed to give my search engine indigestion. Shorty + Apocalypse: nothing promising here either. What about Shorty + millennium as a last throw and then beddybyes?

Shorty + millennium, seeking. Shorty + millennium, found. Whole string of results this time, but it was result number three that caught my attention. And how.

MILLENNIUM MADNESS:
BLAME IT ON DENNIS THE SHORT.

'The new millennium,' said the site, when I entered it (trying my best to look calm, because meanwhile I had switched to the common-room computer: you never knew with sites, how safe they were, at least I didn't), 'starts on January 1st, 2001. It did NOT begin on January 1st, 2000.'

Yes, well, I'd heard that one before. Usual old round-the-mulberry-bush debate. I read on, without the rider to what I was reading really sinking in until I'd finished. The key part of the article went like this:

Dennis the Short, or Dionysius Exiguous to give him his Latin name, was a Scythian monk who created our modern calendar system, based on the birth of Christ, in the year AD 532. Since he was operating without a zero, and also for neatness sake, in order that Jesus could be one in year 1 and two in year 2 and so forth, Dennis began his system from year 1 instead of year 0. It is therefore a matter of straightforward counting to establish the correct

144

date of the start of the new millennium. In fact
there is no argument to the contrary, or not outside
the slack perimeters of popular credence: the US
Naval Observatory, Royal Greenwich Observatory,
Encyclopaedia Britannica, Library of Congress,
National Institute of Standards and Technology,
World Almanac, etc. etc. -- all give January 1st,
2001 as the correct date.

Had I checked out Shorty at last? The right Shorty? Well, it looked as if I had. And it looked too as if I'd have been better off if I hadn't. What did all this amount to? Easy and ghastly: it amounted to the fact that, if the reckoning was correct (and I could see no fault in it), there was a virtual certainty that the murderer would kill again, that the organisation would strike again, this year round.

Perhaps they had made a wrong calculation in predicting the birth of the Antichrist in December 2000? No, I don't think they had, I don't think they were that stupid or that slack. I think it more likely, ruthless as they were, that they had decided to leave nothing to chance. In which case baby Lulli, poor baby Lulli, would have died for a cavil, a quibble, a small-print clause brought in to placate the more traditional elements in a hyper-traditional bunch. One extra dead baby, what difference did it make to these unscrupulous lunatics? None. The vital thing was to parry Spoiler.

And where was Spoiler – the next Spoiler, the most likely one? He was on his way again: biding his time, cocooned safely in his mother's womb, lapped around by amniotic fluid. Sucking his thumb perhaps; I've heard babies do that, even before they're born. Curled up trustfully, waiting to enter a world where pain and death awaited him like a couple of vultures, virtually on the threshold. If he was to be born on Christmas Day he must be fairly ready now, maybe his head was already pointing in the right direction, locked in his mum's pelvic basin or wherever. Oh, my renegade God, oh, my sweet, cruel Saviour – first You abandon me on the rocks of disbelief and now You wash up at my feet this dreadful bundle: the prospect of another crime, involving yet another innocent creature. What do You expect me to do, all alone and nothing but my nut to help me?

When's the next lunar eclipse after Christmas? How long have I got to monkeywrench the project? And where's my wrench, and how do I set about using it?

Idiot, you've just answered that one yourself: your monkey-wrench is your blooming monkey nut. No other tools, no other ammunition, no helpers, no nothing. So, put that nut of yours in a vice and twist it till it cracks. You've been sitting around on your rump, fiddling with the problem as if it were a crossword and you had all the time in the world in which to solve it. 'Sooner or later. I'll get to the bottom of it sooner or later,' with a tacit aside to yourself that the later the better. Adam *told* you to hurry, for goodness sake, but, no, you paid no attention, you thought that was just him being chippy. And now *look* where your laziness has landed you. The earlier shit-pit was the Cloaca Minima in comparison: *this* is the Maxima, this one here, and you are in it up to your quivering nostrils.

*   *   *

A month. Twenty-nine days to be exact. The next lunar eclipse after Christmas fell on December 30th and today was Saturday 1st: I had twenty-nine days in which to act.

But where was I to start? And when I said 'act', what did I mean? Act how? Act where? Against who? (Or should it be whom? Couldn't even decide that.) Oh, Adam, you got me into this mess: now, if you're anywhere within earshot or thoughtshot or wishshot, for pity's sake come and get me out.

Hi, Benevolent. No panic. Think it through. You have to act as a shield, right? As a buffer between the baby and its would-be killer. Up till now you've been floundering around trying to identify the murderer – correctly? Incorrectly? *Well, we shall see – but when you think of the problem logically, as a conjunction that you've somehow got to prevent from taking place, then it's sufficient (and much, much simpler) for you to identify the child. The enemy also has to do this, of course, but that's his look out: the only important thing is that you make sure you identify the same baby he does. That settled, the rest is easy.*

Is it? Are you sure?

Piece of cake. You are in possession of vital information: you know the date the killing must be carried out in order to be effective, you just said it: December 30th, 2001. You know the time, or you can find it out from the NASA material on my discs. How long does a lunar eclipse last? Couple of hours, sort of thing? Three? Four? Well, you must find the baby and stick with it, by hook or by crook, for as long as the eclipse lasts, and make sure no harm comes to it.

Why did you say hook like that? By hook or by crook?

Oh, come on, it's a way of speaking. Your nerves are in a bad way, poor old Benzedrine. Just calm down, eh? You're sitting pretty: the enemy knows someone has entered the lists now, but he still doesn't know it's you, and that means you have a fair advantage over him – for as long as you keep it that way.

I'll keep it that way all right, just watch me, champion pussyfooter that I am. Why didn't you do the same, Adam? Or did I ask you that already? Why did you confront him face to face? Why, for heaven's sake, when you knew how dangerous it was? Why?

Ah. Why? Ever heard of pride? Ever heard of intellectual hubris? My downfall in both senses. Don't let it infect you, Ben. Seriously. I mean this. Don't talk to the monster, whatever you do, and more important still, don't listen. When you come near him, as in the end you must, stop your ears like Ulysses did his crew's against the sirens. Understand? Shout, make a noise – anything to swamp the sound, but DON'T LISTEN TO HIS CONFOUNDED WORDS.

Why? What's so terrible about his words? What could he say to me of such dire import that you don't trust me to hear it? Words are only words; it's his deeds I'm afraid of.

Deeds. Ummm. Fiddlededeeds. Fiddledy, fiddledy . . .

Adam? Are you there, are you listening? What's so terrible about his words, eh?

Adam?

Adam?

*   *   *

Identify the baby, then sit back in an armchair with your feet up and eat your piece of cake. Really. Adam was so flippant now he was dead, so superficial. No help at all; you'd think he enjoyed being out of the picture and watching me, in the thick of things, flail around in circles like a pinned moth.

Identify the baby. Which baby? Why, the baby that the enemy is going to pick out as the Antichrist, of course. But which baby is that? There aren't any babies as yet, there are just pregnant mums, waddling round Rome, awaiting their time. How can I guess the enemy's thought processes when I don't even know for certain who he is? What do I do, pad around after Pascal and Michael, and see if they in their turn are padding around after pregnant women or visiting antenatal classes?

Antenatal classes. Now there was a thought. Did either of the hospitals run antenatal classes for their expectant mums? And if so, would it be a good idea to . . . To do what? A *Tootsie* drag act? Stuff a cushion up my jersey and take part in them? Chat up the mums? Now, dears, let's all stick together – there's a mad, religious baby-killer at large, tracking down the Antichrist who is due to come into the world on Christmas Day this year, so if any of you – sorry, any of us – happen to give birth early that morning . . . Oh, it was hopeless. I was hopeless.

When exactly should this unfortunate baby be born anyway? Last year they had engaged a journalist to find out which was the first baby out after midnight. Was that just a ruse to convince the journalist there was a story there, or did that mean that the Antichrist is automatically the first baby born after midnight, and vice versa? Was little Lulli in fact the first? (You can find that out from Rossi, simpleton.) Or was he simply the first that fitted the criteria? And if so, what criteria?

Back to the files: – Male. (Yup, for certain: the enemy was nothing if not traditionalist.)
– So probably Jewish male, by the same token. Semitic anyway. (Was little Lulli Jewish? Check again with Rossi.)
– A head wound and a near-death experience. (At birth, though? Or could these come later on in life? Unclear from text.)
– Extra-white teeth. (Well he was unlikely to have any teeth to begin with, so that was no help.)
– Sparkling eyes. (All babies have those.)
– Pale eyelashes. (Like Adam's. Not sure, but I think they all have those too.)
– A flattened finger or toe. (The famous 'Mark of Desolation', or 'Sickle of Desolation', as it is sometimes called.)
– A smell of wine or vinegar on his clothes. (Nappy smell, not much help either.)

Summing up, the only reliable criteria appeared to be sex and the sickle; even race was problematic.

I spoke again to Rossi over the phone to find out the two missing details on baby Lulli. No go. He had forgotten practically everything in the meantime. Or else he had grown suspicious of me. Or else – worse – the enemy had got in touch with him again and put the wind up him. The name Lulli meant nothing to him, he said (but it did before, I remembered that clearly), and, no, unfortunately he had taken no notes. When I asked him whether the phoney magazine had wanted data on all the infants born that Christmas night, or just the firstborn, he hedged a bit, saying he couldn't remember that either, but under a bit of pressure finally admitted they had in fact wanted the full list – not that it had been very long: roughly three names in all, four at the most. Parents' surnames, addresses, anything he could gather on either side.

At this point I expected him to ask me why I was so curious – it would have been the normal reaction, no? – but the weird thing was, he didn't, he just sounded desperately anxious to put an end to the conversation. So I rang off, not much the wiser and badly rattled: I felt the enemy's fingers everywhere. Rossi was another direct link. What if they rang him back and asked him if anyone had been in touch with him? OK, he knew me as James, but still . . . my voice, my accent, my way of speaking . . .

Should I pick up the phone again and ask him not to tell anyone I had called? Or would that make matters worse, and should I . . .

Oh shove the lot. And first and foremost shove fear. Adam was right, sooner or later I was going to have to lock horns with the enemy; I might as well get used to the idea. Up till now fear had served a purpose, and still did, in fact: it kept me careful, and being careful kept me alive; but a time would shortly come when it would be an encumbrance, and in preparation for that time I must learn to shed it now and again. Throw it off. Polish up another persona. Fear is positive for spies and fugitives; it's a fat lot of use to gladiators in the arena.

That's the spirit. Yell, Benzai! and at 'em. Good luck, Gladiator Ben.

*   *   *

All wrong, my calculations now that I had switched objectives: no good looking for a child until it's born. Including Christmas Day itself, therefore, I would have, not twenty-nine days, not twelve or

150

even seven, but a scant six for the finding and saving of the baby. OK, God managed to create the universe in six days (and that was pushing it a bit, from the results), but for a mortal like me working on his own it was not enough. No way, no way. I desperately needed a helper.

But who? I played – no, I did not *play* – I fretted at length with the idea of enlisting either Phil or Paola Serra, and finally, with a whole host of worries and reservations – more on her account than mine – settled for Paola Serra. I trusted Paola on instinct, why couldn't I let myself hope in her just a bit on instinct too? Mind you, I didn't *want* to involve her in anything so dangerous or unpleasant, didn't even want her to know anything so dangerous or unpleasant was going on, but provided I could keep her out of the action and cook up a convincing explanation for her as to why I needed it, I thought with her help I could manage – just about. I didn't have the enemy's resources: I couldn't cover two hospitals at the same time, but with Paola keeping an eye on the happenings at the San Giovanni for me I would be free to concentrate on the other, the San Giacomo. John and James, both brothers taken care of.

What could I tell her, though? How much could I tell her? How much should I tell her? And *where* should I tell her? To meet her in the hospital itself might be fatal. Time was drawing in, the enemy might have his Black Riders out already. Someone might see us together and twig. On the other hand, it would be difficult to find a reason for us meeting anywhere else – especially with the jealous husband in the offing. That was all I needed, thank you very much: a jealous husband plunging into the fray as well.

In the end I decided to re-employ my sleuth technique: hang around in the café on the island with my eggcosy drawn well down, and wait till she came off her shift. Or maybe wait in the church. Have another little word with the crucifix there. I had plenty more to say to it.

It would play havoc with my studies, but who cared. My work was going to the dogs anyway, and even if I had a future I couldn't see it as being in orders – not after this rough ride. Quite what I'd do when the ordeal was over or where I would find a niche for myself, I couldn't imagine. My brush with the priesthood had branded me, marked me off, the way I knew it would, and the mark was indelible: I would never again be quite at home in the secular world. I could foresee money as posing a bit of a problem too: at present I was like royalty in that respect but soon I would need to earn some; I couldn't sponge on Mum indefinitely – think of the power it would give her. Yet who wants a faintly poofy priest manqué, orphaned of his God, with his credo in a shambles? Who would know what to do with one? And who would be prepared to put one on the payroll, even if they did?

Ah, well, time to worry about these things later. If there *was* a later. Which, unless I could think up a plausible story to tell poor unsuspecting Paola, one that would justify my asking her for help, but wouldn't scare the wits out of her or expose her to risk, there easily might not be.

Antichrist lore came to my help here. Antichrist lore and Roman superstition. I discovered, from one of the library books I consulted on the subject, that until recent times it was known practice in Rome for male babies born on December 25th to have the sign of the cross etched on the sole of their foot. A precaution against their being either taken or mistaken for the Antichrist. The book described the practice as barbarous, but I reckoned it was still one up on circumcision.

This was the spiel I eventually trotted out for Paola. For once all went off as planned: I caught her coming out of the hospital and we went and sat together on the embankment of the Tiber and lit up a couple of fags while I put my case forward. I don't go in for smoking much but I thought it would act as a bond. And it seemed as if it did, she couldn't have been friendlier. I have a hunch – oh, dear, I do have that effect on women sometimes – that I stirred up her maternal instincts. She certainly patted me on the back in a motherly enough way when my smoke took a wrong turn. There was this oddball in college, I told her when I got my voice back, not a priest but a fellow student (it sounded less dramatic that way, somehow, more of an undergrad's prank). He had this fixation about the coming of the Antichrist, which according to him was due to take place in Rome this Christmas, and he was determined to seek out the baby that best fitted the bill and to safeguard it from the Devil's powers by scratching it on the foot with the sign of the cross. Nothing serious, just a scratch, but all the same I wanted to put a stop to this stupid business if I could, and in the quietest, no-fuss way imaginable.

Paola listened while I went on to explain the details, dragged deeply on her cigarette with a macho bravura I couldn't help admiring, and tapped the side of her head with a free finger. She didn't look particularly surprised by what I was saying, and I guessed that, like Patty, she had a lowish opinion of the clergy, me included.

I think I was right. Priests, she said to her cigarette butt in a searing voice when I'd finished speaking, before flicking it into the river and starting to smoke mine. And they're meant to give us guidance. Last chaplain we had here used to shoot at copulating cats with an air gun. Ah, well. Cruelty was OK, it was the sex that bugged him. Why was I telling her all this, anyway, why didn't I report it to the Rector? What possible help could she be? There'd be panic if she alerted the mothers or the staff or anyone, and on her own . . .

Panic, exactly, I put in quickly. Panic was just what we wanted to avoid. This Antichrist nutter – he wasn't a bad chap in other ways, just a bit squiffy in the head on this particular subject, a bit *toccatino, capisci?* and it wasn't up to me to judge him, or betray his confidence, or ruin his chances for life. He might become quite a good priest in the end, you never knew. It took all sorts. No, I reassured her, she didn't need to get involved, all I wanted from her was basic information on all the babies born in the hospital on that particular day – Christmas Day – starting from the last stroke of midnight on the 24th to the last on the 25th: names, times of birth, parents' names, addresses, telephone numbers, and any background information she could come by. Yes, either about the birth, or about the family, anything. What to do about the matter afterwards would be up to me. If any baby looked to be in – no, not in danger, there was no danger involved – but let's say if any baby looked as if it might be a candidate for the nutter's attentions, then maybe I'd have a word with the family myself, or maybe – yes, well, she was probably right, maybe the Rector would be the right person to turn to in the end.

Paola agreed to all my requests without raising any objections (although I remembered afterwards that she did raise an eyebrow a bit, and both her shoulders, which should have warned me). The way I'd put it, hers was a fairly unobjectionable task. I gave her my e-mail address to send all the info to and we parted on a laugh at the expense of humanity *in toto*. The moment she was gone, however, the laugh died on me. I hoped I hadn't done anything rash. By way of a die it was small, hopefully harmless and hopefully useful, but like all dice once it was cast it was cast. And it was cast. As with the sending of the e-mail message to the college, there was no recalling it.

Allez, alea, give us a six. Two weeks now to Christmas, and virtually nothing else I could do in the meantime except keep a wary eye on Pascal and Michael and a bas-relief profile myself, and try to stay healthy and functioning. My stomach was giving me terrible trouble – I think I was developing gastritis – but I didn't dare do anything about it. I wanted no one, not even a doctor, to pick me out as an individual. I wanted film-extra status, I felt safer that way.

I could tell the enemy was casting his net: I could feel the swish of it coming closer and closer with every day that passed. He must have been looking for the sender of the message ever since it had arrived, and what with my friendship with Adam and the fact I was absent during that crucial Saturday mealtime, I would have been high on his search list. I hadn't noticed anything amiss with my computer yet, but, judging from odd complaints I heard circulating in the common room regarding shifted files and missing e-mails and what have you, I suspected that several students' computers had already been vetted. I kept my programs clean as whistles, and luckily my software was old and unsophisticated, but all the same . . . I wasn't that brilliant on the innards of a computer: what if there was a way of getting at the backup of the recent documents file, for example, and seeing *all* the files I'd consulted, not just the last dozen or so? Those names – WHORE, ECLIPSE, SPOILER and so on – they would seal my death warrant. Oh, idiot, why hadn't I thought to rebaptise them before use? As a safety precaution I laid aside the PATRISTIC HERMENEUTICS altogether. I was tempted to go one step further and wipe all the stuff off the discs as well, but I didn't like to. You never could tell, there might be material there I would need to consult later on. It also crossed my mind it might be a good idea to change their hiding place but in the end I thought better of this and left them where they were.

Mistake and double mistake, because I'm not the only one to have read the Father Brown story about the hiding of the cross. But there you are, and in the end I suppose, in a confused, wiggly way, the mistake turned to my advantage. The vital thing was the purging of my computer, as that trail would have led straight to me, with no mistake and no wiggles whatsoever.

In fact, on the late evening of Saturday 22nd, – and, yes, Doctor McSceptic, *of course* it was done purposely, what better time to catch me zapping? – the bell for fire drill rang. I should have known they would do something like this. Almost simultaneously I heard Michael's voice in the corridor outside: 'Everyone out! No dawdling! Come along now, look sharp!' He even had the nerve to put his ugly muzzle round my door, and I think I caught a kind of smug look on his face when he saw that I was sitting at the computer. Exactly where he wanted me to be.

'Chop, chop, Ben.' I hated that expression: chop, chop. Where had he got it from? He wasn't budging either, cunning devil. I desperately wanted to take a kind of mental photograph of my desktop, and of the computer screen too, so that I would have something to check against when I came back, but with him peering at me from the doorway it wasn't possible. Even a suspicion that I was playing for time, and I'd be lost. All I could do was unobtrusively whisk a few biscuit crumbs under the nose of my mouse with my little finger as I switched off the computer and leave it at that.

Drill that evening seemed to take for ever. Our floor had to file out down the back escape and wait at the bottom in a group, so there was no way I could work out who was missing overall, and whether it was in fact Michael who had stayed behind to meddle. Although I was almost 100 per cent sure by then that it was. My new room neighbour, Nicholas, didn't help matters either by talking to me all the time and asking me questions in an eager, piccolo voice. He was a nice kid with freckles, from a hugely posh background that turned Father Simon on no end when he heard about it, and for some strange reason he seemed to have developed an admiration for me, uncannily like the one I had felt for Adam. Funny how, as you go through life, the same patterns seem to repeat themselves, but in ever fading colours. Another moonstruck priestling with another offhand mentor, busy about his own affairs, only I wasn't half as interesting as Adam was, and Nicholas wasn't even as interesting as me. Carbon copies, growing fainter and fainter as their distance from the template increases, that's what we were.

'I say, Ben. Isn't Hegel a terrific challenge? I mean . . . do you read him in the original or what?'

'Wow. That's pretty impressive. Wow.'

'Ben, how do you translate Geist, exactly? I'd screw up even over the title.'

'Oh, I see. Oh. Yeah. 'Course.'

'Ben? D'you think . . . well . . . sort of way-out reading is dangerous, if you know what I mean? D'you think there are some things you just shouldn't read, ever? Or d'you think . . . ?'

'Ah. Never thought of it that way. Mind if I make a note of that?'

'Oh, I see. Never thought of it that way either. Sorry. Terrible prat. Sorry.'

'Ben? Have you read Rorty?'

Nicholas, Nicholas, tread carefully, I could break your priestly heart. Snap: the way this dreadful duplicate business breaks mine. Should I go and hide the discs in my little admirer's cupboard overnight, then, to make the pattern complete? No, I would spare him the hassle. And I would also – shucks to the Fates – vary the pattern a little by staying alive and out of the enemy's clutches. It struck me here, and not for the first time either, that in order to do so I ought perhaps to take out some kind of insurance policy, like investigators do in films when they hit on a perilous secret and you see them stuffing all the gen into a packet and then mailing it to the press or to a lawyer or someone – or leaving it in a postbox and doing something fancy with the key. How could I manage this, though? Who could I send my packet to? Father M. back in England? The family solicitor? James? James, probably would be best: 'Dear neglected friend, Keep this safe for me. Open only in the event of my death.'

Only flaw: knowing James, he'd open it on the spot and laugh his guts out. Which would piss me off so dreadfully, even if I was dead, that I reckoned it best to forget the whole business.

When at last I got back to my room there were no signs of anyone having fiddled with anything. Computer was cool, files appeared to have remained unopened, all the stuff on my desk was, as far as I could see, exactly as I'd left it. However, however: the biscuit crumbs were *no longer under the mouse's nose* but had been scattered to the side of the pad as if by an impatient hand.

'Or by a draught, Ben,' comments the Doc, when I get to this part. 'That is eminently possible, is it not?'

Finicky old codger. And he's got his adjective wrong too: probability has degrees, possibility doesn't. (Or does it?) But, yup, it's possible that it was a draught all right, just as it's possible – logically possible at any rate – that the blanking mouse ate them.

AND THE EVENING
AND THE MORNING
WERE THE FIRST DAY

Apropos gladiators. I'd always thought the worst moment for them must have been when they left the shelter of the backstage waiting rooms and stepped out into the blare and glare of the arena in full cry. Bloodstained sand underfoot, bloodthirsty yells from the crowd, scary noises-off from hungry felines, blinking eyes, knocking knees, and nothing but your trembling self to rely on.

But I think I thought wrong. Judging from my experience with my own private feline, the worst time of all was the waiting. Time closed in on me like a press, crushing me, crushing me, and the tighter it closed, the more unbearable the pressure became. I felt on a par with the unborn child almost, as if it and I were travelling through the same tight obligatory channel: its liberation would be my liberation; together, after untold lonely struggles, we would see the light.

What would I do when Christmas morning finally came? Let me try and think. Should I wait for Paola's message to come through first, or should I leg it straight away to the San Giacomo and check the births situation there? Probably better to do the second. That way I'd have the alternatives laid out before me and could set about choosing between them.

But then? When I'd chosen? (Assuming I managed to identify the child on Christmas Day itself, in theory it could take till midnight and beyond.) Blank. I couldn't even think that far ahead, let alone plan. In the back of my mind somewhere, I could feel a sort of spontaneous urge towards total sincerity. To leave aside strategies and half-truths and simply go to the parents, whoever they might be, tell them the whole absurd story and beg them, whether they believed it or not, to stand guard over their baby for the crucial four hours of the eclipse. (It was a penumbral

161

eclipse, I had checked, lasting from half-past nine in the morning, local time, to half-past one in the afternoon. So it wasn't even as if they had to keep a night watch: just Sunday morning and Sunday lunch.) Any young married couple would do as much, surely? I mean, they might turn me over to the police, OK, or they might ring up the nearest psychiatric hospital and have me carted off, too bad, but they would still heed the warning I'd given them, wouldn't they, on the off chance . . .?

Or would they? Say they were out-and-out sceptics; say they just laughed. No, I couldn't risk it. Better to keep my own counsel, stay in the shadows and do the guarding myself. But how could I get near enough to the child to guard it effectively? I couldn't. Better the parents, then, sceptics or otherwise. Oh misery. Hard to think it through. So much depended on factors I couldn't possibly foresee. That no one could foresee. One step at a time was all I could hope to take: one calm, reasoned, resolute step at a time.

*　　　*　　　*

Calm, reasoned, resolute – some hope. By the night of the 23rd I was so electrified by tension that if you'd put a bulb in my mouth I think it would have shone. Or maybe even fused. As if the unbearable wait itself were not enough, two additional bad things had happened that day, bringing me two steps lower in my descent. Not many further depths to plumb, you might think, but, no, not for nothing is the pit called bottomless: there was plenty of downhill scope still, plenty.

The first thing that happened was this: in the morning Pascal was taken off to hospital for an urgent operation on his prostate gland. As if. As if. The effrontery of it beggared belief. And where was he taken, to which hospital? Why, to San Giovanni all'Isola, of course. Their man on the spot. I never got round to checking the name of the doctor on whose advice he was admitted, but I didn't need to. Muzzi wangled it, you could bet your last lira;

Muzzi wangled it the way he wangled the urine samples. (And in the end it served no purpose, so Muzzi can urinate off.)

Upshot: the enemy was there, in pole position, in the larger of the two hospitals, and I wasn't anywhere – yet. What sort of plan would have been arranged for the other hospital, then, the San Giacomo? An inside informer probably – another untraceable Sister Whatnot from Wherever, to be planted *ad hoc* and just as swiftly uprooted afterwards. I couldn't possibly compete with such an outlay of forces and there was no use trying. But I could spike the project all right, oh yes, even a little lone fellow like me could still spike the project. *If* I kept my nerve.

The second thing that happened was the discs. Late that evening, knowing sleep was out of the question and thinking maybe a little extra mugging up on Spoiler-spotting might be useful and fill in the time, I went into the empty computer room to fetch the discs from their usual place, and they were NO LONGER THERE. Disappeared, vanished, all three of them. I didn't dare rummage around much or show surprise, or even linger long in front of the shelves, just in case – no, it was ridiculous – but just in case someone had rigged up a hidden camera, or even, I don't know, hidden a pygmy nun in one of the cupboards to act as a spy. Shouldn't wonder if the organisation ran to a few pygmies as well. However, a quick scan was quite enough: the discs were gone. Deliberately removed. One disc could have got out of place, or even have been borrowed by a bona fide user for that matter, but not all three. I grabbed a computer game – one with a train on the front, I didn't know what it was but I'd seen Nicholas play it sometimes at weekends – and left in a flap.

Relax, Ben, relax. It meant nothing. The discs could convey no information about their user: all they could say was that there *was* a user, here in college, and that was a fact that the enemy presumably knew all too well.

But I couldn't relax, especially not my long-suffering stomach. Say there *was* a camera there? How many other people would have taken discs out that evening? And how many in the middle of the night? And how many would have gone straight to that particular spot?

Enough of that. Where was my Russell Crowe persona, and why wasn't he stepping on to the screen with his net and trident? It was about time. Only one day now to go.

*   *   *

December 24th, Christmas Eve. Ergo Antichristmas Eve as well. How I spent the night I remember, fuzzily, but what did I do during the day? How did I get through those tail-end, endless hours? How did I survive the last terrible squeezes of the press – or the ones I had figured and hoped would be the last?

Ah, yes, I helped decorate the tree in the shelter, that's what I did. Broke three glass balls, I was so nervy, providing great merriment: endless quips based on the word '*rompiballe*', which, it was flatteringly agreed, didn't suit me half so well as it did Don Rocco. I was hoping to see Peppe there, or even Stella herself, which was chiefly why I went, but the only visible star was the lopsided one that we made out of cardboard and tinfoil to crown our decorative efforts. I must have spent at least a couple of hours there all told. More with the bus journey. And confession, too, I went to confession at some point – that took up a bit of time.

Oh, the grisliness of those sham confessions with Father Daniel since I had begun suspecting him of collusion with the enemy camp. (And yet I had to go through with them: I couldn't afford to raise even a puff of suspicion that I suspected.) I find it cringeworthy enough listening to myself talking of intimate matters with McShrink, who is a) a person I trust, and to whom b) I tell the truth, or most of it, or try to. Imagine the interchange when these two conditions are missing, not to mention faith in the Sacrament. Imagine the bluff, jovial, outgoing American, huge and pink, and false as a set of dentures, convinced I am experiencing serious difficulties with my errant Eros. And imagine me, the snarled-up, ingoing Ingo, unable to deny the fact but unwilling to discuss it – particularly with him.

That day was even worse than usual. At a certain point Father Daniel asked me how things were going 'libidowise', and I was so floored by the adverb that I chanted back flippantly before I could stop myself, Libidodumb.

Sorry? said Father D. What was that, sorry?

Me: Um . . . Nothing.

Father D: No, Ben, you said something. I didn't quite catch it. Libido dumb, was it? Ben? Let's get this straight: you accuse your libido of being dumb?

Me (deeply regretting my folly): Inarticulate mumble.

Father D: Stop punishing yourself like this, Ben. All bodily drives, libido included, are value-neutral till we act on them. Remember that always. Your libido's not dumb, and it's not smart, it's value-neutral. We've been over this before: there are so many ways these feelings of yours can be funnelled into a positive outlet. It's like energy – heck, you can make a bomb with it or you can run a power plant. I sometimes think Saint Paul himself . . . Well, no, I'm just freewheeling so don't quote me, but, heck, there must be hundreds of holy people . . . thousands . . .

And so our wires went on crossing. I was genuinely curious to know what percentage of homosexuals Father Daniel estimated to run in the saint population compared to the overall, but another mumble seemed safer. As soon as I credibly could I nabbed my penance and departed – technically in peace, my sins forgiven.

(Rhetorical query to the cosmos at large – I expect no answer since there is none: WHERE IS PEACE? AND WHO CAN FORGIVE ME NOW?)

Compared to the day, the night was easier. Clearer in my memory too. I played the computer game all night long from the end of Midnight Mass onwards, and was thankful for it. I got really into it in the end. Funny how a brain only has room for so many ideas at a time, no matter how important they are. I'd decided to check my e-mail at frequent intervals just to see if

Paola was feeding me through any info yet about the births, but the bell for lauds caught me still fighting with the evil Milena on the roof of the Trans-Siberian train as we hurtled together through the steppes. Must get her – just one more try; swipe her with the barrel of the musket and then duck.

Perhaps that's what I should be doing with my days now instead of jabbering away to McShrink or beating my head against the wall and screaming futile questions like the one above: playing computer games. It'd work out a good deal cheaper too.

*   *   *

Christmas morning. The end of the waiting period. Action at last. Now, Ben, now, Russell, gird your gladiator gear and go.

Check for the message first. Nix. Never mind, it'll come through later. Skip breakfast, dodge everyone, slink out of the college and take a bus straight to the centre. How are you going to play it at the hospital? Depends. Probably best by ear. Could pose as a journalist, could pose as a priest, could pose as a journalist-priest . . .

Could pose as a prisoner. They were waiting for me almost literally outside my door – Father Quentin, who stands in as resident psychiatrist, despite his degree being in something quite different, and Father Lawrence. The latter perhaps chosen for his size. In case I showed resistance.

'Ah, Ben, the very fellow. Mind coming along with us for a sec? The Rector's anxious to have a word with you. Just a quick word, but leave your coat . . .'

We've got a nice trendy straitjacket for you instead. I thought it was Michael who'd betrayed me, I thought he'd traced me through the discs. Then for one awful moment I thought the Rector was party to the plot, and curtains. But the moment he started speaking, or, rather, the moment I began to see, through the mist of generic waffle, what he was driving at, I realised it must have been Paola.

166

Great concern about my tiredness. Recognised how hard I had been studying, how tough the second-year syllabus was. Don Anselmo very pleased, incidentally, about my overall progress, it seemed I had been turning in well-up-to-standard work, particularly lately. So, no, no need to look so worried, the reason he had sent for me was not to criticise my academic performance at all, if anything the opposite. Ha, such an unusual thing for him to have to say he hardly knew how to express it, but he was going to ask me to take things very easy for the next couple of weeks. Have a bit of a break. Have a few words with Father Quentin now and again as well. Little chat, sort of thing – quite informal and only if I felt like it. Read a few light books, mingle a bit more with the other students. Solitude *not* always a good thing, concentration neither, you could have too much of both. OD on them, wasn't that the way to say it nowadays?

Was it? I frowned at him. A child's life was at stake: whatever this was I must handle it very carefully indeed. I must appear puzzled and affronted by these aspersions on my nervous state. Not panicky or hurt, which was closer to reality, but coolly puzzled and coolly affronted.

For the moment I was indeed the cooler party: the Rector looked as if he was sitting on a thermal pad. Shift, shift, and a lot of pulling at his collar to let the air in. Mind if he asked me a few questions? No, because – hard to put it – maybe a misunderstanding – certainly an explanation somewhere – but the thing was this: he had received a complaint from the administrative department of a large Roman hospital, to the effect that someone from this college had been upsetting a member of their staff with strange stories; and he, the Rector, had reason to believe that this person was me. Now, wait, wait, wait, he had the utmost faith in my integrity, and if there was any truth in this rumour he was sure it was only a consequence of the stress I was under, but he must ask me straight out: had I in fact been to this hospital – the one on the island – the San Giovanni whatever-it-was-called? I had? Ah. And had I spoken to one of the nurses there about religious matters? Ah, I had? And had I given her a false name? Ah, I had. Ah.

Ah.

Ah.

I wondered how many more Ah's he was going to say. I said nothing myself because I didn't know how far Paola had betrayed me, and didn't want to worsen matters by revealing things that she had omitted. Obviously I must have scared her: she may even have thought the Antichrist nutter I spoke about was none other than myself, and that I needed the information about the baby so that I could get busy with my penknife or scissors. But would she have reported this to her superiors, knowing they'd almost certainly tell the Rector? After patting me on the back and all that – would she have sold me out?

Only one more Ah. Ah. Well, that was it then, that was all he wanted from me: a candid admission. He didn't want anything else. No details. If I had erred, I knew myself in what way, and if it was the nurse who was at fault, misinterpreting, overreacting and generally making a typically female fuss over nothing, then it was no business of ours. He only hoped I had not been acting in jest, that was all.

Good. Now there was just one thing more and then we could regard the matter as closed: I must give him my solemn word that I would keep well away from this hospital in the future. To avoid any further unpleasantness, I understood. The administration had made this request and he had assured them on my behalf that I would comply with it. So? Was that a deal? Did he have my word?

Not yet he didn't because I was speechless. Not to go to the hospital? It cut the ground from under me. It was the worst thing that had happened yet. How could I ever find out about the baby if I couldn't go to the hospital? I would get no news now from Paola, that was for sure; if I couldn't make enquiries on my own account how could I possibly find out what I needed to know? Oh, what a torture chamber they were shutting me into. What *was* I to say? What *was* I to say? Quick, quick, the Rector's bland, forbearing smile was already fading at the edges, what was I to say?

Use Pascal as your excuse, you ninny. He's there, no, in the hospital? Say you have to visit him. Take him some poisoned broth or something while you're about it. Go on, it's worth a try.

'Um . . . Father, I . . .'

'Yes, Ben?'

No, it was no good, it would never wash.

'I . . . I . . .'

'*Yes,* Ben?'

Incaprettato again, only this time it was the baby who would suffocate. The baby, the baby – who could save it now?

'I . . . Nothing, Father. Of course, Father, I give you my word.'

        *   *   *

Judas cracked. Judas hanged himself on a tree with purple blossoms: one of God's ugliest handiworks and one of His loveliest, joined together by a traitor's rope. His last thought is anyone's guess, but my guess may be a bit more informed, given my track-record: Why me, Lord? That's what I think it was. OK, I know it had to be someone, that's the role and that's the script, but why me, why me?

I haven't cracked yet, I haven't even singled out my tree, but the question is there already, hammering around the inside of my skull like an oncoming migraine: Why me, Lord? Why me? Why me?

And then, seeing as there's no answer, I think: Why turn to the Lord, and why ask Him the question? Time I grew up. And *stood* up, and stopped jabbering and kneeling. And/or jabbering and lying on a couch. Time I took responsibility for my actions on to my own two shoulders and looked myself square in the mirror and said, There, Ben, that is what you did and that is what it has turned you into – like it, loathe it, but anyway, whichever, belt up and lump it.

So, on with my *via crucis*. The waiting before the promise was painful enough; after the promise it was agony. I knew there would be no messages from Paola, but all the same I couldn't help dipping into my e-mail about once every forty seconds – just in case she had relented and sent me the information. It was pointless, but there seemed to be nothing else that I could do. A promise is a promise, and a promise is binding.

Or is it?

Remember Socrates and his example of the madman to whom you promised, in saner times, to return a knife you had borrowed, and who now wants it back in order to commit a murder? That promise was no longer binding, according to the dialogue, because a life depended on your breaking it. Same with me and my promise: a life hung on my breaking it. Quite apart from which, there was the other hospital, the San Giacomo, which wasn't even included in the promise. Stay away from *this* hospital, the Rector had said, meaning the one on the island, the San Giovanni. If he'd meant all hospitals he'd have said so.

Ergo, eggcosy and away. Time was limited and precious and dwindling fast.

I had surprisingly little trouble making my escape. I had more than half-expected to find another pair of warders outside my room, ready to collar me and prevent me from leaving the college altogether, but the corridor was empty. In the hall downstairs a depleted gaggle of students stood in front of the noticeboard, chatting and swigging coffee looted from the breakfast table. Hiya Ben. Hiya. Hiya. Among them Inigo: *Ave, Benedicte, Christus natus est.* (*Et Antichristus, Inige?* I felt like asking in reply but couldn't trust myself with the vocative.) As I passed through the gates Felice, the gatekeeper, looked up from unwrapping a hamper and waved. *Buon Natale*, Benny. He always called me that, he was a great Benny Hill fan so I think it was meant as a compliment. *Buon Natale.*

The bus took ages coming. *Natale* was not so *buono* in Rome in the transport respect. When it finally arrived I climbed on amidst a whole crowd of other passengers – most of them decidedly un-Roman, if turbans and kaftans are anything to go by – and jostled my way to the middle where the exit was, ready to jump off the moment we struck via del Corso. Which is probably why I didn't see him. But no sooner had I touched ground than there he was, right behind me and now drawing alongside: Phil. The Rector's bloodhound and my guardian angel.

'Going anywhere particular, Ben? Mind if I come too? First Christmas on me tod like this – no fuss, no family. Feels funny, dunnit?'

He was a bad actor. A good man – I was certain about this now, I could tell from his unhappiness with the role he had to fill – but a bad actor.

'Scrap it, Phil,' I said. There was no point in either of us pretending. 'The Rector doesn't trust me, does he? That's what it is. He's put you on to me because he doesn't trust me. What's the score? You tag on and then report back? Or tag on and try to dissuade me from going where I want to, or what?'

Phil shrugged and opened his hands. I don't know why but the gesture somehow told me that he would be a fine priest one day: his palms looked generous, apostolic, made to help and to bless. 'Report,' he said unhappily. 'I'm to stick by you and then –' (another shrug, another still wider opening of his hands before a sudden drop) – 'say where you went. Sorry, Ben, but he's dead worried. We all are.'

Yes, we all are. But more than worried, I was desperate.

'And you *will* report, of course?' I said, looking at him hard. 'No good, I suppose, asking you not to?'

'Oh, Ben.' He shook his head.

'No good asking you to lose track either? Just for a while, just for, say, half an hour. It's vital, believe me, I can't explain but it's vital, give me half an hour . . .'

The head went on shaking. A sad, tolerant but at the same time Rhadamanthine shake – heaven only knows what warnings about me the Rector had put inside it. Poor Ben, he needs help, he's close to breaking. Well, I did and I was, and it showed, and I was suddenly past caring. That stubborn good-doggie shake did something, jammed some mechanism in my will that no other obstacle to date had managed even to affect. This was it. I had come to the end of my powers and the end of my struggle. I had tried and I had failed. I couldn't go to the hospital – either hospital – and start asking questions about newborn babies, not with Phil at my elbow noting and recording my every word. I simply couldn't do it: I would be breaking my promise to the Rector; I would be out of the college and off on the next plane. And without the questions I had no information, and without the information I had no chance of foiling the enemy's plans and saving the baby.

Hard luck, little baby. I am sorry, I am heartbroken, but I can do nothing. Nothing.

Nothing?

Nothing.

Nothing? Are you sure?

Oh well, maybe, who knows . . . Scarlet O'Hara *docet*. Maybe the day after tomorrow when the offices opened up again I could go to the registry office and dig around for certificates . . . If Phil was not still on my tail, that was. Maybe, maybe, but for today I was beat.

It must have been written on my face, this last bit.

'Look, mate,' Phil said, shifting his feet around as if he'd trodden on chewing gum. 'Look, I'm at sea here. I don't know what's up, I don't know where you were planning on going and I don't want to know, right? All I know is I've got to stick with you. I'm sorry if this fouls up your plans, but that's the way it is. You're stuck with me and . . .'

'I have no plans,' I said. And it was true: all the busyness inside my head, the to-ing and fro-ing and shunting and linking and criss-crossing of thoughts, had stopped, bang, like that. My brain felt entirely still. It was not displeasing, in the way that watching a turned-off telly is not displeasing: you can't very well sit there and slate programmes when there aren't any, just a blank grey screen.

'Oh,' said Phil and did another shuffle. 'Well, I know, what do you say we pop into the shelter, then, eh? Right now, ahead of schedule, and lend a hand. They'll have their work cut out with the Christmas lunches – Don Rocco will be pleased to see us, for one.'

It wasn't a bad idea. Might as well be there as anywhere. 'I didn't sign out for lunch, though,' I said, remembering this. 'Did you? Will it matter? Anyone mind?'

'Mind?' For the first time Phil gave me a proper head-on look and a proper smile. 'You're deranged, mate, remember; I'm on a special mission; and Pascal is out of the running altogether – who's gonna mind? Come on.'

Chance? Providence? Or, as the enemy would have me believe, the Devil looking after his own?

DO NOT SIN
AGAINST THE CHILD

The shelter had a befuddling warmth about it. Although I scarcely needed fuddling, I was pretty spaced-out already. Drink rules had been waived, or at any rate slightly bent to accommodate a crate of beer or two, and a festive, boozy smell wafted in the air, resting on springs of tobacco smoke and stirred by a vague current of anarchy.

Don Rocco welcomed us like a castaway sighting a rescue party. Not that there was much actual skivvying for us to do: cooking and serving had been taken over for the day by a group of young voluntary workers – mostly pretty, upper-class females from the looks and sounds of them – and they fluttered around like so many good fairies ministering to a group of goblins. Or like songbirds feeding cuckoos: dainty and stressed. But for this very reason things were evidently slipping out of control. Words pinged to and fro that I never heard used there before – *Sgnacchera! Bonona! Cosciona!* – accompanied by slurping noises not exclusively or even obviously addressed to the food. Someone had found a spare guitar and on our entry began strumming the umpa-umpa bass used for the famous Roman *stornelli*, or drinking songs, which as everyone knows have a habit of spiralling smutwards fast.

'Get a game going, lads,' Don Rocco urged, rushing forward to meet us. His fisherman's jersey was strangely short, and I noticed a giggling group at one table busy winding a ball of wool: I think they were unravelling him. 'Come on, look snappy, get the cards out, do something or we'll have a problem on our hands.'

Out of the corner of my eye I had already spied Peppe, and my heart did its usual little quickstep just at the sight of him. Slow, slow, quick quick, slow. I longed to go over and ask for news of Stella – how she was faring with her friends (the *Punk Bestie*, the

Italians called them, from their habit of lugging around animals with them everywhere), and how the pregnancy was coming on and everything – but it wasn't the right moment to abandon Don Rocco: his hair looked a bit deconstructed too, Struwelpetery; he was definitely in need of our support.

So, what with *scopa* and *scopone* and bingo and rummy and all the rest, I wasn't able to talk to Peppe properly until late afternoon, by which time he was on the point of leaving. I helped him into his floppy overall coat, dusty from the furniture-restoring job he'd just landed and much too light for winter-wear, and we walked together to the mouth of the underground (underground or underworld? Where was the ball of string leading?), Phil footing along discreetly behind us. The official beer in the shelter hadn't run to much, but Peppe positively reeked of the stuff. There must have been a cache somewhere. No wonder things had been so jolly.

'How's Stella?'

He lurched against me and chuckled. A slightly bitter chuckle. 'Oh, f-fine, considering. I'm on my way there now, if they'll let me in. Just a quick visit, you know. Say hello.'

I'd always thought the San Lorenzo crew kept open house. 'They're picky are they, nowadays, about who comes and goes?' I asked, thinking that they were probably right to keep a bit of a check on people, after the Genoa business, and all the terrorist threats.

'They sure are,' he said, and made a faint attempt to free himself of dust. 'P-poncey lot. This coat won't go down too well, that's for sure, but it's all I've got.'

'Don Rocco's ladies might find you another one if you ask,' I said automatically. Then I stopped and thought. Poncey crusties? OK, the world was changing fast, its social groupings blurring into one another, the way Pasolini foretold, but . . . poncey *crusties*? 'What do you mean, poncey?' I asked. I couldn't see Stella adapting very well to a poncey set-up. Why did she stay there, I wondered, if this was the case? Why didn't she leave? And why, for that matter, didn't she come back here? 'Poncey how, Peppe? Poncey who?'

'Oh,' Peppe said vaguely, 'the lot of them. They're all p-poncey, from the first to the last. But she can't very well leave, can she, not until the baby . . . You know . . .' He flapped his sleeve to free his arm and bent it towards his chest in a cradling gesture.

I saw his point. Pregnant women probably get sort of broody, nest-inclined.

'Mmm. When's it due, exactly?' I asked. 'What date?'

'Due to what?' Peppe looked slightly fazed. The beer, taking its toll. 'Oh, I see, you mean, how long's she going to stay there?'

'Yeah. How long?'

I've been concentrating a lot recently on chance and design, free will and predestination and the like. It seems to me that the key that will let me out of this prison – always admitting that there *is* a key – must be lying there somewhere, in the thick of that tangled old briar-bush of an argument. This conversation I was having with Peppe, for example – why didn't it just wind up the way it had started? We'd nearly reached the Metro by then, why didn't we say goodbye to each other after a few more blurry, beery exchanges and leave it at that? A few weeks, I suppose, Peppe could have said in answer to my question, and I could have said, Ah, and then, Well, give her my love, won't you? And he could have said, Sure, and then, *Ciao*, Ben, and I could have said *Ciao*, Peppe, back, as he staggered down the stairs to the tube station or Pluto's caverns or wherever, and that would have been that.

Instead the x factor intervened, with the value for x being, say, anywhere between 1 for purpose and 0 for happenstance, and he belched and scratched his head and said he hadn't the faintest idea how long, but he presumed it depended on how long they wanted to keep the baby in the incubator.

My shock must have been legible even through the beer haze.

'What?' he said, blinking. 'So you didn't know? I thought everyone knew, it was on the flipping radio. F-f-flipping publicity

179

stunt. You can say one thing for Stella, she never does things by halves.'

My head had been subjected over the past months to various jolts, producing churn-ups of varying gravity in the poor thinking apparatus within, but this time, I swear, it felt as if someone had put an emulsifier right inside my skull and switched it on to full speed. Panic seized me; I could barely move. In fact I didn't move, I half collapsed, right there, on the steps of the Metro, with people pushing by me and stepping over me. Peppe seemed poised for flight – street wisdom: if there's a problem of any kind, run. But I had a hold of his sleeve and wouldn't let go. Too many things I needed to know – all dependent on the strength of the coat material, which fortunately was good, thin but good.

Yet most of the things, in a funny subliminal way, I knew already, because all I had to do was to consult the list of the happenings I most feared, and tick them off in my head as Peppe said them: last stroke of midnight; first boy child; centre of the Holy City – deep, deep shit, and no apologies. Stella had given birth to a baby boy in the early hours of that morning, Christmas morning. On the doctors' calculations – Stella's own were too vague to count, Peppe said she didn't even know who the father was, let alone when it was conceived – the child was nearly two months premature. Her drug record was responsible. The pains had come on during a pacifist protest sit-in outside Saint Peter's, and the actual birth had taken place in the ambulance on the way to hospital. Or even before it had got under way, if Peppe's account was exact.

Which hospital? It hardly needed saying. The San Giacomo, of course. It would be, it had to be. (How long can the chance thesis stand up to this battering, I wonder? How many sixes can you throw in a row before you start baulking? Twenty? Thirty? A hundred?) Not the San Filippo, not the San Camillo, not the San Anyone Else where we would have fought on level terms, more or less, but the San Giacomo, where the enemy's pawn was already in position, backed by a ruddy knight and a ruddy bishop. And that was no mere metaphor.

As if all this was not enough, there was the 99 per cent, no, 100 per cent certainty that the enemy was already fully informed of what had happened and where his victim was to be found. The radio business. Thanks to the Monty Python nature of the delivery, with the dog, that Stella had apparently refused to let out of her sight, tied to the front of the ambulance, barking its head off, and her crusty friends crowding round the back, checking the logos on the medicines and oxygen cylinders and whatever for black-listed brand names, not to mention the chants and the candles and the riot police on their horses behind the columns and the Pope within spitting distance and the rest – news of the event had been broadcast, on national radio. Well, hardly surprising. Probably Vatican Radio had got hold of the story too, but that was immaterial: one bulletin was all it took.

The only thing that kept me from diving into the underground that instant and heading flat-out for the stop closest to the hospital was my knowledge of the time restriction. However much it scared me and tormented me to think of Stella and her baby lying there, virtually at the mercy of the maniac, I knew that for the time being anyway they were safe. He wouldn't strike till eclipse time. He couldn't, on his own reasoning, strike until eclipse time.

Blessed Virgin, Holy Mary, Mother of God, Star of the Sea, Queen of Heaven – if You don't exist, You won't be there to mind what I say anyway, but if You *do* exist, oh if You *do* exist, forgive all my faults and stay with me through this trial. Don't You hide with the moon, don't doze off, don't relinquish Your power, not yet, not yet. Stay with me. See that no harm comes to this baby. Give me strength.

*   *   *

I had waited so long, become so disgustingly professional at waiting, I waited again. Like your Robert the Bruce, Adam, your Scottish arachnophile hero. But a miserable quaking little spider, mine, with a thread so thin, so thin, it would hardly trap a gnat, let alone . . . Oh, better not dwell on that side of things, better not dwell. I could go straight to Stella, warn her, try to convince her, prepare her for our battle, but it was too risky. I might be seen and identified, and that would be it. On the other hand, if I waited till the very last moment and *then* acted, I might just, just pull it off. Storm tactics: they afforded me a tiny chance, the only one I had.

Those last four interim days, those last five interminable interim nights – how did I get through them? I did, that is all I know. Adam maintained that there's no mind/body divide, but I'm not so sure any more. Because I think I stepped out of my body, I think that was how I worked it. I let it go on walking and talking and filling the place in the world it had so far occupied, so that nobody would see anything different in its behaviour, but inside it I was no longer there. I was suspended in some time-governed but spaceless dimension, alone with my thoughts and my fears and my tiny rag-end of a plan: to go to Stella on the morning of the eclipse, tell her everything, and somehow, some-how, the two of us together, or if need be on my own, keep her baby safe and out of range of the assassin.

From my internal fastness I kept covert watch over the fellow members of my community, Michael in particular. He came and went a lot – ostensibly ferrying papers and whatnots to Pascal in hospital for signing. What was he really doing? Where was he really going? I could only guess, but it wasn't that hard to figure out: he was paying visits to the other hospital, the San Giacomo, liaising with the organisation's plant there. Planning elimination, planning infanticide.

How do you kill a baby that is safely housed in an incubator – a modern incubator, with sophisticated monitoring systems, watched over by trained personnel by day and by night? Well, how do you slaughter thousands of people in the heart of Manhattan, armed with only a bunch of paper-cutters? Any-thing is possible if you are mad enough and driven enough, anything. You could jam the monitoring system, for instance, disable it, together with the alarm system, and then send the incubator temperature soaring. You could send a commando group in with poison gas. You could place a poison gas ampoule in the incubator itself, for that matter, fitted with a time device. In fact, lacking moral ones, your only limit is your imagination.

Ben Robot, Ben Golem, a walking husk. A beer-drinking husk, though: I relied heavily on beer to see me through. Perhaps I ought by rights be writing a beer paean now instead of this confession: wind apart, it brought me nothing but benefit. Oh, the blessed cushion that it set between me and my pain, me and my worry. No wonder the desperate stone themselves with whatever's going, no wonder.

When my day of reckoning finally dawned – and almost the very *moment* it dawned, I had to move fast, I couldn't possibly afford to be intercepted again or trailed by the faithful Phil – I left the college, armed with nothing except a strange, last-ditch, can't-be-worse-than-this chutzpah, which settled on me the moment I got under way. Abandoned the college is perhaps the phrase: I thought it unlikely after this last desertion that I would ever be re-admitted, except to pack my belongings, and maybe not even that. And maybe better so.

The eclipse was due to begin at 9.25 a.m. and 4 seconds, and to end at 1.33 p.m. and 2 seconds, reaching its high point at 11.29 a.m. and 2 seconds. The seconds were important, every one of them: a shot can be fired in a second, a knife can be wielded, a poison can be given, a life can be extinguished. Allowing time to talk and time to act, plus a little extra for unforeseen delays, I reckoned I ought to be at the hospital by half-past eight at the latest.

In actual fact I was outside the front entrance by twenty-past seven, but I had to wait till eight to gain entry. This I did by simply walking round to a side entrance and strolling purpose-fully in with the flux of arriving staff. Don't flounder, Ben. Don't show any uncertainty, don't ask any questions. Follow the signs to Maternity and just keep walking.

As I walked, it suddenly struck me in a wave of panic that I didn't know Stella's other name, her surname. Nor did I know for certain whether, the baby being in an incubator, she would in fact be sleeping in the maternity department at all or whether she would be elsewhere, in a special room. For that matter I didn't even know if the incubators were situated in Maternity. Perhaps they were kept separate. Keep walking, stupid, follow the signs, don't look lost, don't look as if you don't belong. If you were in a film you'd snatch a trolley and trundle it, or don a white overall and a stethoscope and bustle around like a medic, and no one would be any the wiser. You'd be resourceful, you'd blend.

But on my thesis, which I still think is correct, the priestly caste is like the police that way, its adherents don't blend, they look conspicuous whatever they do, whatever they wear. Especially, I suppose, if it resembles an eggcosy. I got as far as the glass doors leading to the maternity unit, and there I was stopped. Accosted. Rumbled. Another cardiganed bustlebody, so like Paola to look at that she had me blinking for a second, spotted me through the glass and straight away poked her head out and waved a thermometer crossly in my direction, shaking it sideways like a metronome.

'No visits,' she said. 'Come back later. We're busy. No visits till ten.'

Ten was too late, ten was in the death zone. Courage, Ben, you'll never stand up to a murderer if you can't stand up to a matron. 'I'm not a visit,' I said, my Italian grammar deserting me.

'Oh, no?' She looked even crosser. 'Then what are you?'

A priest, I should have said straight out at this point – what was a lie, after all, when I was preparing myself for a kidnapping and maybe worse? – but for some reason this particular lie was untellable and I mumbled instead something less barefaced about having been sent by the hospital chaplain to act as his stand-in. Same thing really, but not quite.

'Which chaplain?' she snapped.

'Don Gianni,' I said, throwing out flat like a Frisbee the first name that came into my head. Any further hesitation would be my undoing.

'Ah,' she said. 'Which is he? The one with the beard?'

'No,' I said, 'he's the sort of . . .' And with my hands I made a set of semi-circular movements, as if tracing the outline of a bank of cloud. I don't know what prompted me to do this, but anyway it seemed to have the right effect.

'The fat one?' she asked, slightly mollified.

I nodded.

'I see. And what did he send you for?'

My voice was steadier now and I thought I could risk countering her authority with some of my own. 'To hear a confession,' I said, firm, verging on the solemn. 'There is a young woman called Stella Something-or-other – I forget her surname. It seems she's anxious to take holy communion and has asked . . .'

Wrong move. The woman looked furious again.

'Really,' she huffed. 'Really, it's impossible to run a ward under these conditions. The Patient Charter is all very well but there's a limit. Who is this Stella anyway? We haven't got any Stellas here, not that I know of.'

I described Stella's special circumstances, which were indeed so special as to rule out confusion with anyone else. The woman listened, eyeing the thermometer impatiently as if from metronome it had now become a watch.

'That'd be Maria,' she said briskly, well before I'd finished. 'Maria Cennaro – she's the one you're after. Funny . . .' She frowned. 'I had an idea she was Jewish, I don't know why.'

'Er, no,' I corrected her quickly. *Was* Stella Jewish? Idiot, I hadn't thought of that. A slip that might cost me dear.

'Well, no, obviously not, if she's called *you* in,' the woman snapped again. 'Anyway, the mother will be here in a minute, she always comes early, so you can talk to her about it. I've got no more time to waste. You can wait here, I suppose, till she comes.'

And with a grudging gesture she opened the door a little wider and then turned and marched away down the corridor, calculating it nicely so that the glass panel swung back right in my face.

I took it as permission to enter. Which I did, double quick. First hurdle cleared. The all-important thing was now to find Stella immediately, before her mother turned up on the scene. What was the name the matron had mentioned? Cennaro? Well, Signora Cennaro would complicate matters dreadfully. Stella knew me, trusted me, she might believe me; her mother definitely would not.

I waited till Bossyboots had rounded the corner at the end of the long, gloomy corridor, and then slowly began to make my own way down it in her wake. A row of doors stood on either side, mostly with pink or blue rosettes over their lintels, and most of them fortunately open. Ignoring the unmarked ones and those with only pink rosettes, I began poking my head round each doorway in turn, scanning the occupants' faces, in search of Stella's. Now that I was in possession of her family name I felt safer somehow in my quest, more authorised, less of an intruder.

I had always heard, from the hospital-visiting crew in college, that there was a great sense of solidarity in Italian hospitals between patients, and I began to discover it was true. 'Cennaro?' I ventured at the third doorway. The two women inside shook their heads, but instead of just leaving it at that, one of them got off the bed where she was sitting and came towards me, extending a hand.

'Moretti,' she said, smiling. 'Here we're Moretti and . . . Sorry, what's yours again?' she asked, turning to her room-mate.

'Porcu,' said the other woman sheepishly. *(Oh, little gladiator mine: a sheepish porker. I hope you wield that trident better than your pen.)* 'By marriage. But we're thinking of changing it now for the baby's sake.' Then she turned to me. 'Which is this Cennaro you're looking for? What's her Christian name? Has she unloaded yet? Are you the husband, or what?'

Unloaded? Oh, I see. 'Um, yes,' I said. And then quickly, 'No, no, no, I'm not the husband, I'm just a friend, but I urgently need to see her. I'm sure you know who I mean – she's called Stella, at least I call her Stella, but her real name is Maria, and she's kind of small and . . . er . . . frail and . . . and, er, yes, grungy-looking. Definitely. Grungy-looking.'

Both women's faces lit up and they laughed. 'We're all pretty grungy-looking here,' the chatty one said, 'till we can get to a hairdresser, but I think I know the one you want. The one there was all the fuss about in the papers, no? The one with the baby in the incubator – the premature baby that nearly died?'

My heart started beating fast. It was all I could do to keep my voice steady: it seemed to want to race with the beats. 'That's her, all right, that's Stella. Could you tell me where I can find her? Which room she's in?'

The woman stepped outside with me into the corridor and put a helpful steering hand on my arm. 'Special Care Unit,' she said, and had just begun explaining to me the route I must take when a tall figure in a long overcoat brushed past us with a gentle apology.

My guide stopped in her tracks. 'Why, there's the mother,' she said, delighted. 'I'm sure that's the mother, she can take you there. Wait.' And before I could restrain her, she was shuffling off in her slippers after the overcoat, calling out in a loud purposeful voice, '*Signora! Signora! Un momento, un momento.*'

The figure paused and turned. That day was a day of surprises, most of them terrible, but this one, strangely, was not. Quite the contrary. The figure turned and, guess what – I found myself looking into the slanting, elfin eyes of my idol, Fanny Ardant.

Well, not the real Fanny Ardant, of course, but there was little to choose between them, and I'm not sure, had it come to a choice, that my scales wouldn't have tipped slightly in Signora Cennaro's favour. I was stunned. A tiny part of me, still receptive to such feelings, was enchanted as well. I had never thought of Stella as having such a mother, or coming from such a background. I'd always known she came from Naples, but somehow the picture I had built up in my foolish, trite imagination was of a backstreet tenement with washing strung from the balcony, and scooters scooting noisily below. An overworked, under-educated mother, a brutish, unemployed father, squalling siblings – the classic family for a girl like Stella to want to escape from. But evidently, if escape hers was, it was from something rather different.

'*Si?*' this vision of elegance said, tilting her lovely head to one side and looking, not at the woman who had addressed her, but directly at me. Almost as if – no, that was wishful thinking on my part – but almost as if she found me a worthy object of attention. '*Si?*'

I'm not sure what my own course of action would have been, had I been left to make the reply myself, but the decision was made for me by my helper/hinderer who at this point intervened again, telling Stella's mother who I was and what I wanted.

Signora Cennaro's eyes had never left my face, and didn't do so now. She went on staring at me hard, thoughtfully and carefully, like someone judging the weight of a pig at a fair, and tilted her head again to the other side.

'A friend of Maria Stella's?' she said.

I swallowed. I was glad she had linked the names for me, and glad that she used the Stella part as well – it felt more familiar. 'Yes,' I said. 'From the shelter, you know. From the days when she was . . . That was where I met her, in the shelter, when . . . Before . . . When she had the puppy.'

With the mention of the puppy, the examination seemed to come to an abrupt end. I appeared, thank goodness, to have passed. From the tilted angle the head dipped downwards courteously.

'The puppy. I see. And you have come to visit my daughter now? That's very sweet of you. Come along then, follow me, we'll go together.'

I tacked on behind her in a slipstream of perfume. I knew I ought to be thinking hard, planning ahead, adapting somehow to this new ingredient, the improbable Fanny Granny, present at my

188

meeting with Stella, but my head refused to clear, and the perfume didn't help, nor the pace we were keeping. We sped along the corridor, round the corner, up some steps, through a second set of swing doors and into another corridor, and finally came to a halt – skidded, almost, to a halt – in front of a small pink formica door labelled Private.

'Here we are,' Signora Cennaro said. '*Eccoci.*' Her smile fell on me like a light beam: I hoped there was no conflict between her and Stella, it would have distressed me no end. 'I'll just go in first,' she said, 'if you don't mind, and make sure . . . The milk business, you know. Oh, I was forgetting – your name?'

'Ben,' I said. 'Perhaps you'd better say Ben from the shelter, in case Stella doesn't remember.'

Oh, that smile again, really wide now, with a touch of the mischievous. 'Ben from the Shelter. *Va ben*', Ben, *va ben*'.'

It was suddenly all so easy. I was there, I was smiled on, I was among friends. Stella would believe me, Stella would trust me, and this bewitching mother of hers, so different from mine it was hard to think of her in the parent category at all – she would trust me too. I had a feeling that, having passed her scrutiny, she trusted me already. She gave off – it was hard to define – a sense of strength, of balance, of total at-homeness in this difficult world. I imagined her as the sort of person who would know how to fix things in a top Paris restaurant so as to get the best table, or on a desert island so as to get the best campsite. Wherever she was, I couldn't see her being at a loss.

All so easy, and then, just as suddenly, a hitch. As we stood there, the pink door opened of its own accord and, bottle in hand, out came the matron, or ward sister or whoever she was, who had first spotted me through the glass. Bossyboots. For a second it seemed OK because she said nothing, merely pushed past both of us with a grunt of disapproval, presumably at our being there so early. But then, cowed perhaps into civility by Signora Cennaro's suave '*Prego*', she paused and turned.

'I see you've met up with him,' she said, 'the priest who's come

189

to see your daughter. That's all right then. But don't let him tire her, *mi raccomando*.' And off she went.

The door stood ajar as she had left it and I could see Stella's feet on the end of the bed, clad in socks with toes. But only for a split second, before her mother slammed the door shut and barred the way, her overcoat spread like a pair of wings. Her face was still beautiful but it had undergone a shocking change. No blood in it at all.

'Priest?' she hissed at me. 'You are a priest, and you didn't say so? What are you doing here, priest? Get out, I tell you! Get out before I call the police. One step forward and . . .'

'No, no, no! I beg of you! I beg of you!' I think I must have sunk down on my knees at this point, like I did in the underground with Peppe, to anchor myself somehow tighter to the ground. I think I came close to blacking out as well: to have come so near and then to be thwarted, it was so bitter as to be unbearable. 'I'm not a priest, I swear, I'm not, I'm not. I'm a friend of Stella's, a true friend, I have nothing but her safety at heart, I . . . I . . . I . . .'

Who knows what else I babbled or what else I did. I must have looked abject, but who cares? Afterwards I found fur in my mouth and on my fingers – moultings, I suppose, from the lining of the coat, so perhaps I latched on to it in my despair, holding tight, refusing to be repulsed. One thing is certain, I must have made a fair amount of noise. Enough at any rate to rouse Stella from her bed and bring her to the doorway. I remember in my confusion seeing the woolly-clad toes again, and then hearing her voice. A few typical laconic barks. A laugh. That snort of hers. A repeated swearword – Stella had no hang-ups that way, unlike me. '*Mamma! Insomma! Lascialo! E solo Ben, cazzo! Ma che cazzo fate!*'

Next thing, I was inside the room, sitting on the bed beside her, being revived with a kind of Ribena drink in a characteristically grubby glass, and the furious Fanny was reclining in a nearby chair, massaging her well-coifed scalp, the way people who have perfect hair do under stress, and eyeing us both sceptically. Oh ho, this persistent little pig needed re-weighing.

I burned my boats – there was nothing else for it. No time, no margins. I set my boats deliberately alight like fire ships and watched them blaze. I told Stella and her mother everything: everything I knew, everything I suspected, everything I feared, including my worst fear of all, namely that they would both find it impossible to believe a word of what I was saying. And then I waited, completely drained of feeling now, for their reaction.

It was surprisingly slow in coming, when you think that I had warned them of the time pressure and it was coming up quarter to nine already. Stella was the first to speak, but when she did, it was not to comment on what I had said but to ask her mother how she was feeling and whether she wanted the window open. She called her *Piccola*, which struck me as strange, given the relationship and the difference in build.

It was true that Signora Cennaro was looking worryingly pale: I doubt she had recovered colour since that first blanching, when she took her stand against me in the doorway, and now her skin was waxen white like a gardenia. Still, I thought it a curious opening on Stella's part. '*Come stai, piccola?*'

Her mother shrugged off the enquiry. 'It's nonsense, of course,' she said, as if not really speaking to anyone else, but just thinking aloud. She took another few precious seconds for biting the skin round all five nails of her right hand, precisely, not missing a cuticle. 'It's utter nonsense. Still . . . This friend of yours, Stella, he may be right: there are people who believe nonsense. People who act on such beliefs. Say things are exactly as he says, what should we do? Alert the staff here in hospital? Call the police? What? Say little Ezra is in real danger . . .'

Stella seemed more shaken by her mother's few sentences than all of mine strung together. She stared at her, astounded, and then banged on the mattress with clenched fists, punch, punch, punch, and came out with her favourite swearword again.

'*Ma che cazzo dici, Mamma? Che cazzo dici?* You're not going to take this seriously, are you? You don't seriously think . . . ? It's madness. What can we do? Ezra can't leave the incubator. What can we do? Oh, sod you, Ben. Oh, *Mamma*, don't just sit there, say something, say something. Oh, sod you both, sod you both.'

Her mother, still wearing her pig-weighing expression, gave a funny low whistling sound.

'Calm down, *tesoro*,' she said. '*Calma, calma.* According to your friend – to Ben here,' and she granted me a sliver of a smile, 'we have a full seventeen minutes left, so there is no need for panic.' (And I thought she'd overlooked the time factor. How wrong I was. But I was right about the weighing.) 'The question is this: we have to weigh things carefully. Risks on the one side, risks on the other. Risks of acting and risks of not acting, risks of believing and risks of not believing. It's four hours, after all, that's all it's going to take, and then it will be over. Now, what is it Ben is asking us to do? He's asking us to remove Ezra from the incubator for a period of four hours in order to . . . Sssssh, sssssh, sssssh . . .' (Stella had resumed her swearing with a vengeance) '. . . in order to save him from what he claims is certain death. We either believe him or we don't, but even if we don't, we're left with a doubt, and the doubt is unbearable. If anything happened, if this conspiracy exists and these criminals manage to . . . No, we could never live with a thing like that. We must go and get Ezra immediately. Now. This very moment. The way I see it is this: we take him – we snatch him – oh, I don't know, we'll work it somehow – and then we hide him somewhere safe, but somewhere here in the hospital, so that we still have the incubator to fall back on if we need it. If he needs it. That way we risk a fuss, we risk him catching cold, we risk a lot of things, but we don't risk him being murdered.'

'We do if Ben's the murderer,' Stella said, with a slightly crazy laugh. 'Honestly, I can hardly *believe* this is happening. It's like a nightmare.' With a bound she was off the bed and grasping around for her dressing gown. 'But I know one thing, I'm going to my baby now, and I'm going to sit by that *fottuta* machine for the whole *fottuta* eclipse and no one's going to . . .'

'Stella, no. Stella, please. Reason with me, please. Trust me, please. Trust my judgement.' Signora Cennaro, incredibly, remained seated and hardly raised her voice at all, just half a tone perhaps, if that. 'I've worked it all out. It's better this way, I promise. We go to the incubator room, all three of us. I distract the attention of the nurse, and you open up the incubator while she's not looking and take Ezra out. No, no, sorry, I'll begin again, I'm forgetting the milk – we can't have him going hungry. First you go alone and grab the bottle from that room they keep it in – you know where it is, you're allowed in there, no one will see anything strange in that. Then we all three of us go to the incubator room; I create my disturbance, and you snatch up Ezra. Right? Then you and Ben together go and hide with him somewhere – probably best in the basement, or where the boilers are; somewhere sheltered, somewhere warm – and don't come out again until the danger time is past. Unless . . .'

'Unless he dies on us.' Stella was in a bad way. She was crying now as she spoke, and she threw the dressing gown on to the floor and kicked at it till it tore. I could hardly forgive myself for placing her in this mess, on this rack. But, you know, attraction has such a weird effect: OK, I felt miserable and guilty, but at the same time I was quite simply chuffed to bits at the thought of spending all of four hours alone in her company, no matter the circumstances, no matter the danger. If fate had so decreed I think I'd have ridden happily beside her in a tumbril. Loon.

HIS EYES SHALL BE BRIGHT

I wish sometimes that McShrink was a bit more Baconian. Or do I mean more Anglo-Saxon, less European? Or just less intellectually frilly? Anyway I wish he'd test my story for truth in a straightforward empirical way: take a plane to Rome, for example, and go to the wretched hospital and see for himself if the wretched boiler room is in fact where I say it is, or not, and if in fact there is an old, dark-red, out-of-use oil tank in one corner with a whole lot of piled-up material on top of it or if there isn't, and whether or not this material includes a fake Christmas tree, long discarded.

That way, he'd know I'd been there, wouldn't he? But no, he's not interested in that kind of straightforward, pragmatic test. And I suppose the airfare would work out a bit pricey too.

So what about a lie-detector, then? Why doesn't he borrow one of those, read the squiggles, see if I fail or pass? I'll tell you why, because for him there is no possibility of my passing ever, that's why. His books are cooked in Freudian sauce. All that a positive result from these tests would prove, to his way of thinking, is that in my madness I'd gone to a great deal of trouble to get my facts right, that's all. Ergo, igitur, all the madder. Not that you can really blame him: if he took this little lot on board then he would have to rebuild his entire belief-bank, from the foundations up. From the foundations down.

But the Christmas tree was there, all right. ('Christmas tree, Ben? Sure you don't want to call it an Antichristmas tree? You've done a lot of this juggling around in recent weeks with Christ and Anti. It would be interesting to work on the significance you attach . . .')

I'd prefer to tell you to go and stuff yourself, Doc, like an Antichristmas turkey. The tree was there, I swear it was, and

Stella and I and baby Ezra were behind it, huddled close together with our limbs and clothes tucked tightly round us. A shoe heel or a piece of hem sticking out from our hiding place, and the game would be up for all three of us. If you can call it a game. Fanny had thrust her fur-lined coat on us at the last moment, as swaddling for Ezra, and it was proving a great nuisance – slithery, bulky, ungovernable – and warmth was the last of our problems: the boiler room was stifling.

Fanny's 'disturbance' had been spectacular. A regular Sarah Bernhardt turn. In fact, I didn't like to mention this to Stella, who had enough on her plate already, but I was worried lest her mother had seriously hurt herself in her striving for authenticity. In a perfect simulation of an epileptic fit she had crashed down in the incubator room like a felled tree – no cheating, no hands, no buckling at the knees, no nothing: just a ninepin topple, whack, on to the bare floor. I could hardly spare her a glance, the baby snatching had to be done so quickly, but in the confines of our hiding place, as in a darkroom, I found emerging on my retina the imprint of her long, thin graceful greyhound frame, stretched out on the linoleum, and a patch of red where the head was – dark as beetroot juice.

Can you apply arithmetic to fear? Are two fears worse than one? No, not if the one is already boundless. I saw this film once, I don't remember what it was called; it was a pretty crappy film, but there was this one scene in it which really struck me. It was a scene of terror: a girl in a cupboard, hiding from an approaching maniac. You didn't see anything, just her face in close-up; and she didn't do anything, just stood there motionless and sobbed and sobbed and sobbed in utter silence. It was awful to watch, and I remember thinking that it was probably so awful because it was probably true, and that that was what people did in moments of extreme fear: stood stock-still and sobbed without making a sound.

We sat stock-still, Stella and I, for what must have been nearly two full hours but neither of us cried, and that was the only difference. Not even when we heard the door creak open, and a series of footsteps tread first in our direction, then back off, and then twist round and come towards us again. Not even when we heard the metal cupboard to our left being yanked open and someone rummaging around among the mops and brooms. (We had thought of hiding there, but Stella had ruled it out on account of the smell of cleaning fluid.) Not even, not even, when we heard the whiffling. Oh, yes, because it was him all right – it was the whiffler. I would have recognised the sound of him anywhere, through any curtain of sound, no matter how strong. At a rock concert. Under a landing helicopter. Anywhere. And here it came to my ears through just a flimsy veil of purring from the boiler.

('If a boiler can purr, Ben, can't it whiffle too?' No, Doc, sorry, it can't, not like that. And what about later, in my bedroom? No boiler there.)

Ezra didn't cry either. Extraordinary for a baby that small. Stella had forgotten the milk pump, and her mother had forgotten it too, we all had. We had the bottle with the extracted milk inside, but just as Stella was about to use it – roughly half an hour or so after we'd hunkered down behind the tree – I suddenly thought, No, *not* the milk! Not *this* milk, you fool! If the killer can't use his hands, what better means than a bottle? and dashed it in panic from her grasp. Just in time. Stella caught her breath, but she knew I was right because she made no protest, merely pinched one of my fingers lightly in hers and let out a little whimper. 'Oh!'

After that we were stumped, or ought to have been, because, I don't know, but I don't think premature babies are much good at latching on to the breast. Why do they bottle feed them other-wise? But there was nothing else for it: Ezra was beginning to fret a little, strike up what threatened to be the prelude to a mewl. If he cried outright we'd either have to abandon our refuge alto-gether or else I'd have to leave the two of them and go back for the milk extractor. Unfeasible. Unthinkable. So Stella struggled with the vest thing she wore instead of a nightie, bared her breast and clapped Ezra to it, and, wonder of wonders, he began to suckle.

I didn't see anything much of this scene – mother feeding child – the light was so dim and I was too shy to take a proper look, but what little I saw hangs in my memory gallery today like a stolen masterpiece. A Raphael, a Bellini Madonna in a gangster's cove. Curve of breast, lesser curve of baby's head in profile against it, minute monkey hand with its fingers working, working in time to the suction of the cheeks, and then a flash of brilliance as the eyelid parts to show a little sapphire eye sheened over with content. I use it like my stills from the soup kitchen, to gaze on now and again and try to convince myself that there *are* good and beautiful things in the world, and that this is one of them. But unlike the soup kitchen scenes it doesn't always work – it depends a bit on the eye.

'Makes me retch, this feeding business,' was Stella's whispered comment. 'Makes your clothes stink of cheese.'

And they say travellers are romantics. I'd never noticed Stella before being fussy about bourgeois things like smells. Myself I found the idea almost too crude and upsetting to contemplate – breast-feeding on canvas is one thing, in the flesh it's . . . well, it's different, everything in the flesh is different. Did my mother ever breast-feed me? Hope it never enters her head to tell me. But when the whiffling started I couldn't help coming back to the subject. Worrying about it. Tolkien again: it felt as if this snuffling creature was literally, physically, sniffing us out. Closer and closer he came. She came. It came. Pff, pff, pff. Pff, pff, pff. Would this smell, the smell of our humanity, our earthiness, our weakness, betray us?

I was tempted to leap out and scream. At least it would have snapped the tension, at least I would have had the advantage of surprise, at least if I'd gone I would have gone out fighting. But I was there for Stella and Ezra: I kept still, like they did, trusting in the dusty plastic foliage; trusting in the fact that it was such a stupid place, no seeker in his right mind would ever bother to check it out.

Not first time round, that is. When, at last, the footsteps receded again and the whiffling with them, and we heard the door creak open again and then close, the first thing I did when I felt it was safe to speak was to tell Stella that we must change hideouts.

'Na,' she said. 'Na,' and curled herself tighter. She was shaking like a rattlesnake all over. Maybe up to this moment she hadn't really believed me, hadn't really taken in the extent of the danger. Now the shock had caught up with her.

'Na, na, na.'

'But you must, we must,' I hissed at her in desperation. 'He'll be back. He'll be back to check again. We must go somewhere he's already looked. I've had an idea, Stella: the cupboard, we must go into the broom cupboard.'

Violent shaking. 'Na-a-a-a.'

'Trust me, trust me, Stella. Listen to me. It's the safest place now: the cupboard. Let's get in there quick, while we still have time.'

'Na.' It was like talking to a catatonic. Shake, shake, shake. Na, na, na.

So with a lightning swoop I took Ezra from her – tore him from her is more exact – and held him high up above my head so she couldn't get at him. He looked amazing, framed against the branches of the tree; his eyes sparkled, as if he was enjoying himself no end. I reckon babies like being held in the air.

'I mean this, Stella,' I said. (Where did I get this resolve?) 'I'll kill him myself this instant, if you don't do what I say and get into that cupboard. Now. Immediately. I'll throw him on the ground, I'll throttle him, I swear I will. You'll never get him back alive.'

'Swine,' she said. 'Bossy, know-all swine.' But she said that later and in one of the kindest voices she has ever used to me.

Because she had been right about the cupboard the first time, and I was right the second. The whiffler came back a bare couple of minutes after we had climbed into it and pulled shut the door. We heard him stalking round the room again, much faster this time, and we heard him banging around with some sort of instrument, maybe an umbrella, maybe a stick. He passed the cupboard without pausing. And you know? This time I wasn't the least bit frightened, I was triumphant, I knew we'd got him beat. We didn't hear him leave for quite a while – it is possible he waited a certain amount of time like that in each room, hoping, if we were there, we would make the mistake of thinking him gone and coming out into the open. Or else he was just getting tired. Or desperate, even: time was playing on our side now, there was only ninety minutes left to go. But when he did leave and when finally we emerged, a football match later (plus the two seconds injury-time: I wasn't risking anything for the sake of two seconds more Vim up Ezra's nostrils, anyway he looked to me to be thriving on it), the first thing we saw, lying at our feet, was the Christmas tree, in three separate pieces: not content with looking behind it, the whiffler had actually pulled it down off the tank and on to the floor, where it had broken up in sections.

Swine, bossy know-all swine. As an expression of gratitude for saving Stella's son I had to be content with that.

Granny Fanny, from under her bandage, was a little more voluble. And a great deal more gracious. Avowals of lifelong gratitude, lifelong remembrance, and a standing invitation to the Cennaros' Neapolitan villa (which I shall take great care never to accept). My first impression of her had been right; even with all those stitches in it, her head had continued to work clearly. How she had held in check the hubbub that Ezra's disappearance from the incubator must have caused, I can only imagine. She said nothing when I asked her about it, merely smiled and gave a wry little nod in Stella's direction, so I reckon she put all the blame on her. Ex-addict daughter, bit wild, bit unbalanced; post-natal depression, complicated by the fact that she can't bond properly with the child when he's in the incubator all the time – don't let's cause her any more trouble until we're sure she's left the hospital, I beseech you; better for her, better for you, better for all of us; I've sent someone in search of her already, before we take any other action why don't you go and help him? That's the sort of tactic she must have used.

Anyway, whatever she did, it worked. When I reappeared in reception with Stella and the baby and the trailing overcoat I was treated by the entire hospital staff as a hero, a bacon-saving hero. Where *had* I found them? Where *had* they been? Everyone had been hunting, they had turned the place upside down and not a trace. How clever of me to manage it when everyone else had failed. Oh, bless the little fellow, he looks fine, he looks fine.

This last, naturally, intended for Ezra. I didn't look so fine, I'm afraid, after our four-hour ordeal in the basement, and neither did Stella. The feeling of triumph that had flooded through me in the cupboard seemed to have remained right there: in the cupboard, with the broomsticks. Defeat may be bitter, but victory is not much sweeter. It was over, the nightmare was over. I had outwitted the enemy (whoever he was, and at this point I didn't much care if I discovered his identity or if I didn't; let him crawl back to his hole and remain there) and all I felt, to tell the absolute honest truth, was tired. Tired, tired, tired, tireder than I had ever felt in my life before, tireder than I had ever thought it was possible to feel. I knew there were hosts of unpleasant things ahead: facing up to the Rector, taking all the flak he cared to fire at me, facing up to Mum and ditto, gathering up the strings of my tangled life and trying to put them in some kind of order before starting afresh . . .

Afresh? In my present state the very word seemed to mock me. Astale was more like it. Before starting astale, astale and atired, atired, atired.

Stella had been put under sedation – light, because of the feeding, but she was sleepy and slightly groggy when I went in to say goodbye. No good leaving my final message with her so I left it with Fanny instead, who was stretched out on a chair beside her, her feet resting on another. I couldn't help noticing that they were bare.

'I know,' she said, catching on so fast to my reasoning she sort of tripped me up mentally, floored one part of my brain and left the other part staggering. 'I know, I've had exactly the same thought: we haven't identified him, so if he's failed now he'll most likely try again, no? At the next lunar eclipse. But you needn't worry about us, we will find ways of dealing with the danger, we will be very careful. When May 26th comes round . . .'

Had I told her that date? I must have done. But when? I had no memory of mentioning dates at all. 'It's not just a he,' I reminded her, 'it's a they. The organisation may be quite numerous.'

She smiled with her eyes, but coming from under the bandage the smile no longer had such a captivating effect, it looked a little jarring. And the voice that accompanied it was downright steely. 'My husband's family is quite numerous,' she said. 'Don't worry, *tutto andrà ben*, Ben. Believe me, *tutto andrà ben*.'

But I think, even without this repetitive word play – not a touch on Adam's, not a touch – I had already started to realise that *tutto* would not go *ben* at all.

THE BOTTOMLESS PIT

For this part of the story there is no truth-test to apply: there are no facts to check against, it is his word against mine. And the lie detector would be useless too: he was lying through his chattering teeth all right, but not in the way a machine would apprehend.

He was standing in the corner when I came back to do my packing. All afternoon spent on, well, you could call them windings-up: a long jaw from the Rector, telephone calls home, travel arrangements; yes, windings-up, and tuckings-in of odd little strands, and windings-down. *Finis somnii*, end of dream and end of nightmare. Relief on all sides, except Mum's. And even she – well, she was getting me back, wasn't she? She was getting her little sooty lamb back. It was dark, so I didn't see him, and I didn't switch on the light because all I wanted was to throw myself down on the bed and sleep, sleep, sleep.

I was about to do exactly this when I heard him. Heard it: the whiffling. I was too tired to feel greatly afraid, my heart just sank resignedly, the way it does, for instance, when you get called to the telephone just as the dinner bell goes, and my body switched wearily back into fear mode. Of course he was there: he'd come to punish me, after what I'd done did I think he was going to let me get off free?

Well, kill me then, screwball. Kill me quick and let me rest. Who are you anyway? Come on out of the shadows and let me take a look at you. Come on, come on, tiger. Here, puss, puss, puss.

But he didn't move, and when I switched the light on I realised why: it seemed I was not the only one to be afraid. Facing me was, not Michael as I had come to expect by now, but our diminutive Vice-Rector, Julian, in the grips of what I soon realised was a mega-attack of asthma, brought on by terror. The whiffler whiffled when he was scared, that was it. His face was white and drawn, the bridge of his nose had that fleshless, sunken look you see on cadavers or the terminally ill, and on either side of it the nostrils beat rapidly like fish gills, flailing for air: Pff, pff, pff. Only, in the case of a real fish, I presume, it would be for water.

What people say in moments like these is bound to be a comedown. Monster! I could have hurled at him, Murderer! Fiend! Anathema! Something dire but dignified like that. Instead I sank down on the bed, turned to face him, and said limply, 'You. So it was you.' And with this passed the oratorical buck: let him do the talking, my word-store was inaccessible.

When he finally got enough breath together to answer, I admit my enemy upstaged me as regards style. Not the words so much as the tone. Unlike mine, his voice was charged with emotion – loathing is what it came over as, loathing laced with terror. (But these are *my* prerogatives, you creep. What are *you* doing with them? Loathing and terror are *my* prerogatives.) 'Tcha,' he said, in this thin, scathing, trembling voice – the sort of voice you'd reserve for a leprous hag who was trying to seduce you. 'Don't try that one on me, Benedict,' (though it might as well have been Maledict from the way he spat it). 'Don't feign ignorance, you knew perfectly well it was me.'

I said nothing, just stared. I was rather fascinated by him, to be honest, despite everything. How *could* he have done what he had done, and now be standing there, quaking like a fragile little Miss Muffet up against a tarantula? How could he square a conscience less squareable than the circle? And how dared he pre-empt my fear, grabbing so much for himself that there appeared to be none left for me, its rightful owner?

'The discs,' he said, making a funny roundish gesture with his thumbs and forefingers that I think passes for something quite different among feminists. Things were getting altogether rather wild. 'You had the discs, so you knew, you must have done.'

'Knew what?' I said.

'That it was me.'

I couldn't follow him. I'd been through those discs with a nit-comb. How could I possibly have missed anything so important as the name of the person I was hunting for?

My puzzlement, however, can't have looked quite as genuine as it was.

'Oh, stop the play acting,' he said, his breathing coming slightly easier now, so that he was able to inject his words with a shot of anger as well. 'Don't take me for a fool. Of course you knew. Shorty. Check out Shorty. Who else goes by that nickname if not me? Who else could it refer to? Of course you knew.'

We seemed to be slipping into a Lewis Carroll predicament, dancing a quadrille on the brink of the abyss. I fell obediently into step.

'But your nickname isn't Shorty.'

That made him start a bit. Had it not been for the gravity of the situation I would have sworn he looked faintly pleased.

'No?'

'No.'

'Ah. Well, anyway, whether you knew or not . . .'

'It's Sneezy.'

'Sneezy?'

'As in the Tale of the Seven Dwarfs,' I confirmed. 'You know . . .' And I began to list their names. In for a penny of absurdity, in for a pound.

'Oh, my God! What are you . . .? What am I . . .? We're not here . . .' He jerked suddenly forward from the waist, like a puppet, and put his hands over his ears. I remembered from my imaginary communings with Adam that I was the one who was supposed to be doing this – blocking my ears. Our positions seemed mockingly reversed, all along the line.

When he straightened up again, all the tension was back, all the . . . Well, yes, it was terror all right, there was no other word for it. Despite this, however, he edged forward now, his eyes screwed up in perplexity, as if anxious to examine me from closer quarters.

I rose quickly and stepped backwards, till I was pressed against the door. A small man, true, but he had got the better of Adam; I wasn't going to let him come within striking distance. Unless of course he had a gun . . .

No, he wouldn't have a gun, he couldn't: these people's methods were more insidious: pushing off roofs, poison, suffocation. 'What do you want from me?' I said, my fingers already twisting at the doorknob.

He stopped in his approach.

'Nothing. Just to see . . .' Then that strange bend at the waist again (stomach cramps? A stitch? Or was he going to vomit?) and an even stranger sob. A prayer: the filthy hypocrite, he still had the nerve to pray, although I took it the second part of his oration was addressed to me.

'My God! My God! Please help me, God, I just don't understand . . . You're as frightened as I am, you horror, you're as frightened as I am.'

An end to this nonsense, it was really sending my compass haywire, I didn't know where we were or what was happening. 'Of course I'm frightened,' I said. 'You killed Adam, you killed that other baby – the Lulli baby – and did your damnedest to kill this one. Why should you spare me?'

I'd said it now, accused him outright of his crimes, but it still sounded like Lewis Carroll dialogue, like *Looking Glass* language, it still didn't sound real.

'I killed?' The verb seemed vaguely to offend him. 'You're wrong there, you know,' he said, 'I killed no one. As a matter of fact, I didn't even know they would . . .' He shook his head, as if to rid it of something, maybe guilt, maybe unwelcome images. 'But there . . . perhaps they had to or perhaps it was a mistake. Anyway, I'm sorry.' (*Sorry*? He was *sorry*?) 'I let them in and I told them where he was, that's all. The rest . . .'

I was about to say something, or, better, do something, I didn't know what, but he checked me with outspread hands and went gabbling on.

'I *trust* them, though, I trust them. They're right, they *know*. I wasn't sure they were right about you, but they've been right about everything else so far. The place, the date, the circumstances – everything tallies with the prophecies. A hundred little details. They're right, they're right, it had to be stopped, we had to stop it somehow. We had to try.'

'With three murders?'

'Murders?' He didn't like that term either. 'One tragic error and two mercy killings, that's all it would have been. A mercy for humanity. He was in Satan's employ, your precious Adam, you know that? He was a forerunner. The child . . .' His voice rose on this last word until it almost cracked into falsetto, and the dreadful bellows of his breathing started up again.

'The child is beyond doubt . . . The child needed dealing with. Still needs dealing with . . . But every time will be harder, yes, thanks to you, every time will be harder. He'll grow, he'll flourish. The girl's father is a top Camorra lawyer, did you know that? What hope will we have against the Camorra? We had a chance . . . we had this one perfect chance, and you . . .'

Gabble, gabble, mutter, mutter. All these reams of lunacy spewing out of his mouth like paper out of a jammed printer. Mother's name, Mary. Her mother's name, Ann. (Didn't know that: Granny Anny Fanny.) A Jewish grandmother on the maternal side, so the child could claim Jewish status too. Peppe, Giuseppe: Joseph, carpenter by trade. (That was nonsense, Peppe had worked as a furniture restorer for the past two months only, and Don Rocco had got him the job.) The humble birthplace, with the animals standing by. (What animals, for goodness sake? I suppose he meant the dog and the mounted policemen. The whole thing was utterly demented.) The vermouth. (*Vermouth*?) Yes, vermouth. Didn't I know that the disinfectant had been seized by the anti-capitalist protesters, and the ambulance men had had to make do with a bottle of vermouth to staunch the umbilical cord? Didn't I know that? And didn't I know what vermouth was? Vermouth was wormwood, vinegar, artemisia – Verm-oud, Worm-wood, and it was written in Revelation: 'The name of the star is called Wormwood.' Wormwood. Wormwood. And the number of the Beast? Don't say that had escaped my notice too? Six hundred threescore and six. NERON

CAESAR: EZRA CENNARO. Same letters, same value: Six six six. Six, six, six.

I couldn't take any more of it. Adam was my friend, I had loved him, and this befuddled brute had killed him, or at any rate connived in his murder. Stella was my other love, and he had tried to kill her baby.

'And you know why you were drawn to these two particular people?' he said, picking up my accusations like hand grenades and hurling them back at me. 'Because the damned *choose* evil, Benedict, of their own free will. Like is drawn to like. They courted you, both of them did, they flaunted their friendship at you like a couple of prostitutes, they . . .'

'That's enough!' I yelled into his hated face. 'Stop it, will you, just stop! Stop!'

And stop he did. I had authority over him. Now that *was* strange. We looked at one another, glared at one another, through a membrane of silence that was still vibrating. If he wasn't here to attack me – and it didn't look as if he was exactly in the fighting arm of the organisation, I believed that much of his rantings – then what in the name of blazes was he here for?

'To understand,' he repeated, when I asked this in those very words. (I noticed he flinched on the 'blazes' – bet it was deliberate.) 'I *have* to understand, whatever the cost, I need to.'

He was filching all my privileges, all the things I had a right to: fear, scorn, loathing, ear-stopping, and now the need to understand. I just couldn't find a foothold on this slippery, marshy ground. I was floundering, floundering.

And without realising it I must have been sinking too, already, deeper and deeper into the pit, at the same speed and in the same way the words were sinking into my consciousness, i.e. slowly but penetratingly and sticking there fast. Would earplugs have saved me? Would anything?

Will anything? Will analysis? Will reason?

The die again. The sixes. How many in a row before you begin to shelve coincidence and look for another explanation? And if you find no other explanation? If is there is none? Even after a hundred sixes, even after a thousand, must you still cling to chance? Can you? 'Adam had pale eyelashes' – so what, so what, he was a Scot, he was fair, lots of Scots are fair. 'He was a disbeliever' – no, he wasn't, he had a probing mind, that is all. He had doubts and he brought them out into the open and examined them; in his own way, he was brave and loyal and coherent – a darn sight more so than many others in this position, who just shut their eyes and pray for faith and haven't the guts to question anything. 'Coherent, you say? Yes, he was coherent all right, you only have to see the blasphemies he wrote. Truth is, he was never a real postulant at all, he was just a stooge of Satan, an evil servant put there to pave the way for . . .' False, false, false – words as false as their speaker.

And yet, false though they are, they stay with me, those terrible closing phrases of my opponent's, before I grabbed hold of him and threw him bodily from the room. That verse from Deuteronomy: 'The prophet hath spoken it presumptuously: thou shalt not be afraid of him.' (Although he was afraid, he was puffing fit to burst now, and I could feel his shoulders trembling in my grasp.) And then his final accusation:

'I thought it was the Scot, I always thought it was the Scot, but I know now: it's you. He was just a minor forerunner, just a member of the cell. *You're* the one I should have been watching out for all along. They were right: *you* are the False Prophet. You, you, you. It's written in Thessalonians: "And then shall that Wicked be revealed, whom the Lord shall consume with the spirit of his mouth, and shall destroy with the brightness of his coming." You! You! You!'

*   *   *

'One up on Napoleon, anyway,' says the Doc, without the slightest trace of a smile. 'I see a strong narcissistic element,' he adds gloomily, 'in this custom-built doom which you imagine is reserved for you in your quality of False Prophet. Would you agree with me there?'

No I wouldn't, no I don't. I see shame. I see shame whichever way

I look. I feel like Kafka's Gregor, like the poor verminous outcast beetle. Mad or bad, take your choice: it still shuts you out of the fold.

Some days – the marginally better days – I opt for mad. I tell myself the whole thing is rubbish: a pile of coincidental rubbish. And to prove it I search for the things that were missing and make a list of them in my head (which in itself is already a pretty strong proof of my madness). Stella was not a virgin, for one thing, demi- or otherwise, very much the reverse. The baby had no head wound, not that I noticed, and I never heard one mentioned either. Jewishness, going by strictly orthodox rules, is not acquired on the basis of a maternal grandmother alone, at least I don't think so. And the famous Sickle of Desolation was definitely missing. (From the baby's hands at any rate. I never saw the feet and I never want to.)

On the worse days, bad runs away with me. Leaving aside the names Anna and Maria, which are so common in Italy you can't really count them (everyone is called Maria, even the men); and leaving aside the Peppe business, which is simply false, and the vermouth, which is rot, I am still left with a pretty indigestible set of facts: a male child of Italian nationality, born in the precincts of the Vatican City on midnight of December 25th, 2001, who has undergone a near-death experience, and whose name, being a pretty close anagram of Nero's, presumably has the gematric value of 666, if you were to work it out. (Unless in the Hebrew alphabet Z and S have different values, but I am too scared to check this, just in case they don't.) All this is nothing, however, when compared to the eyes. It's the eyes, those bright, laughing, sapphire eyes that plague me, and will do for a long time to come.

Those eyes. That eye. Those eyes . . .

Maybe one day the Doc will pull me through: i.e. get me to pull myself together and through. Who knows? *Scientia triumphans.* Maybe I'll turn into a tough old sceptic, shake free of Mum, learn to say the F-word. Maybe. One day. In the meantime each lunar eclipse will see me literally sick with double-edged fear: fear lest they get him, my little blue-eyed Ezra whom I worked so hard to save, and fear lest they don't.

A NOTE ON THE AUTHOR

Amanda Prantera is the author of twelve novels, the most recent being *Capri File*. She was born and brought up in East Anglia and has lived in Italy for many years.